DON'T GO DOWN THERE

KIERSTEN MODGLIN

KIERSTEN
MODGLIN

Cover Design by Kiersten Modglin
Copy Editing by Three Owls Editing
Proofreading by My Brother's Editor
Formatting by Kiersten Modglin

First Print and Electronic Edition: 2023
kierstenmodglinauthor.com

For the women who know.

The human heart has hidden treasures,
  In secret kept, in silence sealed;—
  The thoughts, the hopes, the dreams, the pleasures,
  Whose charms were broken if revealed.
  ...

  And feelings, once as strong as passions,
  Float softly back—a faded dream;
  Our own sharp griefs and wild sensations,
  The tale of others' sufferings seem.

CHARLOTTE BRONTË

CHAPTER ONE

ANDI

Something is wrong.

The second I walk into my house, I know it. I feel it in my gut, somewhere down deep. Bone level. Cellular.

My body radiates from the sensation, as if I'm suddenly an animal in the wild, innately aware of danger.

It's dark and silent in the house, first of all, despite my husband's gray Mazda sitting in the driveway. But that's not why I feel this way.

There's something off with the air.

Something suffocating.

As if I can inhale the stress and the tension, detect them with my lungs.

"Spence?" I call into the still, silent house, flipping on a lamp as I pass through the living room on my way to the kitchen. It's lighter in here, the afternoon sun shining through the bay window, but I still can't shake the feeling that something is very wrong.

Where is he?

I cross the room, place my purse on the long granite top of the island and peer out into the backyard.

Nothing.

"Spencer? You here?"

Back at the island, I reach for my phone, checking to see that he still hasn't responded to my texts or calls. When I received a notification from our location-sharing app that he'd arrived home in the middle of the afternoon on a Friday, I'd initially sent him a text joking about him slacking off.

After an hour had passed with no response, I started to worry.

What if something was wrong?

What if he was doing something wrong?

Images of finding him in our bedroom with a stranger—clothing strewn about, naked bodies melding together—filled my mind.

I'm not an especially jealous person. You can't be when your husband works in the entertainment industry and is constantly spending time with people who spend more on their appearance in a month than I make in a year. Models, actresses, singers... Beautiful women just looking for their break. Though my husband isn't an agent yet, being an agent's assistant still means he's exposed to and constantly around exhaustingly gorgeous people.

Not that he's ever given me any reason not to trust him. Spencer and I have been together for a decade, and we have a beautiful life and perfect children. Our sex life isn't lacking. We're happy. As much as two people who spend every available moment with each other can be happy, we are. Still, it's not like him to arrive home early without letting me know what's going on. It's rare he beats me home at all, frankly. He knows I can see his location, so it would be a major error in judgment to come here without some sort of excuse, but why isn't he answering?

A new wave of panic washes over me.

The image in my mind changes—the woman is gone now, the clothing back on his body, and his chest is soaked in blood. There's blood splattered across our walls, our bedsheets, and the lamps that *almost* perfectly match our taupe curtains.

I squeeze my eyes shut, shaking the image from my head.

Maybe he's just sick. Maybe he came home not feeling well and passed out. It's not unreasonable. Though he would usually give me a heads-up, if he was terribly ill, maybe he couldn't.

I step around the island and glance down the hallway. At the end of the long hall, our bedroom door is shut; the only light in the dimly lit space comes from the kids' bathroom door that's been left cracked open. With quiet, cautious steps, I move toward our bedroom. The carpet conceals the sound of my footsteps, and I listen closely, preparing myself for whatever I might hear—throes of passion, the whimpers of a dying man, or the violent sounds of his sickness.

When I hear none of the above, I suck in a sharp breath and push the bedroom door open.

My eyes scan the empty room—our black-and-white floral comforter is still neatly spread across our bed, the white, double closet doors are shut, and there are still fresh lines in our gray carpet from where our robot vacuum ran last night.

There is no blood. No vomit. No dying husband. No naked woman.

I don't know whether to be relieved or more concerned. "Spencer?"

On his nightstand, I spot the first positive sign that he's actually been here. His wallet, phone, and car keys are resting next to his wireless phone charger. I walk toward the bed and pick up his phone, tapping the screen. There are three text messages and two missed calls—all from me.

I check the bathroom next, but it's just as empty, just as silent. If Spencer is sick, it doesn't look or smell like he's been in here. And he's not in bed. Nor is he in the living room, kitchen, or backyard.

Where does that leave?

I check the rest of the room warily, my heart pounding throughout my body as I pull open closet doors and check under beds.

Is he planning to scare me as some sort of prank? I wouldn't put it past him, though he's not particularly playful. Still, I hope for it to happen. For him to jump out of a hiding place I've yet to check and yell *boo*, to tell me everything's fine, that he's fine, and he just came home early because he didn't have anything else to do for the day.

As I check more places, still not locating him, I can't shake the feeling I had when I first walked into the house, and even before that when he didn't text me back. It's growing worse—more urgent, more certain—by the minute.

Something is very wrong.

I exit the bedroom and cross the hall, pushing open Ava's and James's bedroom doors, though I don't actually expect him to be in either room. The guest room and hall bathroom are also empty.

Back in the kitchen, panic ravages me. I try to slow my

racing heart, to find a way to think rationally, but I've lost all sense of reason.

The worst possibilities swim through my mind: Is he leaving me? Did someone pick him up from the house and take him somewhere? Is he missing? Is he dead? Was he fired?

Where is he?

Where is he?

Where is he?

His clothes are still in the closet. Where would he go without his clothes, phone, or wallet? Or car, for that matter?

Unless he didn't go willingly.

What if someone forced him to come home, forced him to open the safe and give them everything inside it—our gun, emergency cash, wills, and birth certificates?

What if—

CRACK.

I jolt as a sound from behind me interrupts my thoughts.

Spinning around, my eyes land on the door to the basement. Is that where the sound came from?

I swallow, my throat suddenly parched. My heart hammers in my chest as I ease toward it.

"Spencer? Is that you?"

Briefly, I consider calling 911, but dismiss the thought. It's irrational.

Still, I've never liked going down to the basement. When we moved into the house, our first order of business was to have the laundry brought from the basement to the main floor. It's dark and damp down there, the stairs are rickety, and the spaces between each step, combined with the fact that the handrail barely qualifies as a safety measure, freaks me out. It's mostly used for storage at this point, though anything down there has to be kept in plastic storage bins rather than boxes because it floods on occasions when we get a fair bit of rain.

Spencer would have no reason to be down there, but I know what I heard.

Or...I know I heard *something*, more like. A sort of sharp, cracking sound, like a ruler over a desk.

Just once. Like someone knocked something over.

I puff out a long breath, reaching for the doorknob. The last owner painted the entire door black, though he didn't manage to prime it properly, so it's clumpy and chipping in several places. It also has one of those old skeleton key holes, though whatever key may have worked at one time no longer exists.

I'll just push open the door, flip on the light, and call down. It's probably nothi—

"*Don't go down there.*"

I jump with a shriek and check over my shoulder to see my husband standing in the hallway.

"*Jesus!*" I turn around, resting my head against the door, and releasing a loud sigh. "Don't do that! You scared me." I clutch a hand to my chest, trying to slow my breathing. Underneath my palm, my heart pounds as if it's caged in and wants out.

Sweat gleams on Spencer's forehead, the wetness slicking his dark hair down at his temples. His shirt is rumpled and dirty; the knees of his slacks are covered in grime. In his hands, he's holding a small tea towel.

"Sorry. Didn't mean to scare you. I didn't know you were home," he says.

"Where did you come from?" I peer around him.

"I...was in the garage." He points over his shoulder, his face wrinkling with confusion like it's the most obvious answer. I should've thought to check there, but like our basement, our one-car garage is used solely for storage and the tools Spencer owns that are too big to fit under the kitchen sink. "What are you doing home? I didn't hear you come in."

"I was looking for you. I called your name several times. You didn't hear me?"

He shakes his head.

With the adrenaline dying down, it's replaced by a strange combination of relief and anger. He's not sick, dead, or cheating, but he is oblivious to the stress he's put me through. "Why are you home early? And why haven't you checked your phone? I've been worried sick."

He pats his pocket as his eyes dart down the hall. "I'm sorry. I don't have my phone."

It's not an answer or explanation. I shake my head. "Sorry for what? What's going on? Why can't I go into the basement?" Taking in his appearance again, fear creeps in. Why does he look so dirty? "Is something wrong?"

Has a pipe burst? Is the wall of our basement collapsing? Do we have some sort of leak? I run through all the possibilities in my head for why he'd be home and filthy in the middle of the day.

He opens his mouth, then closes it again, drying his hands on the towel. He can't seem to meet my eyes.

"Come on, Spencer. Out with it. What's wrong? You're scaring me."

Placing the towel down on the island, his shoulders slump. "I need to tell you something."

"Okay." A lump forms in my throat like a ball of wet dough. I can't swallow it down. Can't force it to go away.

Something splinters in my chest, a warning of what's to come. A confirmation that I've been right.

Something has happened.

Something bad.

My suspicions, my fears, were warranted. This wasn't just my anxiety talking, making me overthink and overreact.

"Let's go sit down." He points toward the living room before heading that way, but I can't move. It's as if my feet have been swallowed up by the floor. If I try to take a step, I'm certain my knees will give out.

"I'm not going anywhere until you tell me what the hell is going on. Why are you home early? Why do you look like that?" I suspiciously eye the basement door I was just forbidden to open, then turn my face back to him. "What does any of that have to do with the basement?"

Stopping in the doorway between the living room and kitchen, he drops his head into his palms. His next words are muffled, though I hear them all the same, and their weight is enough that I have to grip the doorknob again so I don't stagger.

"I've fucked up."

CHAPTER TWO

ANDI

"What do you mean? What have you done?" My vision blurs as I try to make sense of it, my ears suddenly hot. In my mind, I keep trying to rationalize, offering solutions that won't be as bad as I know it must be—he's lost something, he made a mistake at work, he agreed to a visit from his parents without talking with me first.

His eyes dance between mine, haunted and lost, his mouth drooping open. "It was a mistake." The words come out in a breath.

My body turns to stone, and I realize what he's saying without hearing the confession. I can see the truth of it in his eyes. I square my jaw, my hands balling into fists. "Who is she?"

I wait for him to laugh, to say I've misunderstood, but he doesn't. Instead, his gaze drops to the floor.

"I'm so sorry."

"I need a name, Spencer."

"Heidi," he squeaks out.

Two syllables, five letters, and they're enough to knock the air from my lungs. I steel myself as bitter tears blur my vision. I hate myself for crying right now, for giving him the satisfaction. He doesn't deserve my tears, the bastard.

"Her name is Heidi." He repeats it again. More daggers to the heart. More pain. More *no*.

"You slept with her?"

The silence that fills the room is deafening. It burns my ears, suffocating me, but I can't bring myself to say the words again. This can't be happening.

He wouldn't.

He *wouldn't*.

Eventually, he nods. His eyes meet mine. "She meant nothing to me—*means* nothing to me. It was just sex."

I scoff, looking away. "Did you find that line in the *Cheating Husband's Handbook?* That's what they always say, isn't it? Like that makes it any better. If anything, it's worse. You didn't feel anything for her, and it was still worth ruining our marriage."

"I didn't—" He cuts himself off. "I'm sorry. It was a mistake. A stupid mistake. I was weak. I don't want this to ruin anything."

"Is she someone from work?"

"A client, yeah." He clasps his hands in front of his stomach, running his thumb over the opposite palm. My mind flashes to the parties they have—big, blowout events I often have to miss when Kaylee, our sitter, can't keep the kids.

I picture them—the woman I've now conjured in my mind hanging all over my husband. I imagine them, drinks in hand, laughing it up over how gullible I am.

How trusting.

"Great, so you've just made me look ignorant to all of your coworkers, hmm?"

"No," he says quickly. "No, it wasn't like that. We were discreet. No one at work knows, and it has to stay that way."

I take a step back, shaking my head. "You're unbelievable..."

"Look, I know this isn't easy to hear, and I'm sorry. I didn't want you to find out this way—"

"Why *are* you telling me?" I demand. "Not just because you've suddenly grown a conscience." A boulder sinks in my stomach. "Are you leaving me for her?"

"What? No! Of course not." He reaches for me, but I jerk backward.

"Is she pregnant?"

"No. Nothing like that."

With another step back, I brush against the basement door and turn to look at it. Dread swims through my veins as I look at my husband once more. "Why are you telling me, Spencer?"

His eyes flick to the basement door. "I never meant for it to happen."

"For *what* to happen? The affair or..."

No.

The noise I heard earlier repeats in my mind.

Someone's in my basement.

Don't go down there, he'd warned.

"Spencer..."

"I know. It's bad. It's so bad. I'm sorry, Andi. You have no idea how sorry I am."

"What did you do?" I step backward again, turning to move away from the door.

No. No.

Whatever I thought was going on, this is so much worse. "Why is she here?"

I silently beg him to tell me I'm wrong. Just one small mercy. *Please.*

"I never meant to involve you. I didn't realize you'd come home." His blue eyes swim with tears. "I'm so sorry."

"So, she's down there? Really?" I shake my head, prompting him to tell me I'm being absurd. That, of all the conclusions I've jumped to today, this is the one I've gotten wrong. "Why?"

Running his thumb over his palm again, he glances at the door, locking his eyes on it as he speaks. "She called me at work, said she was coming by because we needed to talk. I didn't want her to draw any attention to us, so I suggested we go to a restaurant, but she insisted we talk somewhere private. I'd been avoiding her..." He looks at me briefly.

I can't catch my breath, no matter how hard I try. My chest rises and falls, but I feel like I'm receiving no oxygen. Is it possible to suffocate without something covering your mouth?

"I was trying to end it. Honestly, Andi, I was. I didn't want to be with her. I was so terrified I was going to ruin everything with you. Our marriage, our family... I would never want to lose what we have. I...I told her to meet me here. It was stupid. Terrible." He looks away, his eyes closing as if banishing the thoughts, wishing away what he's done.

My vision blurs at the periphery, darkening, twisting, and curling like paper burning from the outer edges first. Everything is a blur.

"She confronted me about how distant I've been lately,

and I told her I wanted to call it off, that you didn't deserve this. She just...she snapped. She said she was going to tell you everything, and I panicked. I begged her to be rational, but she was trying to leave, saying she had pictures and videos she was going to send you. I grabbed her hand, just trying to stop her, to make her listen to me, and she tripped. Her head hit the side of the island."

He gestures toward it, and I step away instinctually, searching the icy-white stone for any sign of what he's describing.

"She was bleeding. She had a nasty gash on her forehead, but she was still alive. Awake. She was talking to me, saying she was going to the police. She was going to tell them I attacked her. I tried to calm her down, to explain what happened, how she had it all wrong, but she stepped backward and tried to run. She was confused and dizzy, and she hit the door." He winces. "You know how we have trouble with that latch. She just... She just fell. There was nothing I could do."

I cover my mouth in horror. This has to be a dream.

I'm not awake yet. That's it.

That's the only way any of this makes sense—the only way any of this could possibly be happening.

"Are you joking? Is this some sort of sick joke?"

The scowl on his face gives me his answer before he speaks. "Why would I ever joke about something like this?"

I'm going to vomit. "She just...fell down the stairs?"

"Most of them." His voice trembles as he speaks. "Near the bottom, she went underneath the railing and fell to the floor. I...I think her wrist is broken."

I'm trying to process, to understand exactly what he's

saying to me, but it's ridiculous. It's so utterly impossible I want to laugh, but there's no sign of humor in his wide eyes.

I want to go to bed. No, I want to wake up because this is clearly a nightmare.

"Is she... Is she dead?"

The shake of his head is barely perceivable.

"She's... *She's still alive?*"

He blinks.

"Why haven't you called an ambulance?" I reach for the doorknob, but he steps in front of me. "What are you doing? We have to help her!"

His arm shoots out in front of the door, preventing me from pushing it open. "If we call an ambulance, she will tell the police I attacked her."

"What are you talking about? You can't seriously be considering *not* calling for help. You said her wrist is broken. She's hurt! You can explain to them what happened—"

"It doesn't matter what I tell them. I'm the one who suggested we come here. She's beaten and banged up, and our house is still potentially speckled in her blood. I mean, I've tried to clean it, but I can't be sure I got it all." He huffs. "It'll be her word against mine, and we both know who they'll believe." His voice is firm, and it's obvious he's put a lot of thought into this.

"What are you suggesting, then?" I'm almost afraid to ask.

His hands go to either side of his head with agitation. "I don't know, okay? I was... I *am* just taking this second by second. I wasn't planning for any of this to happen. You know this isn't who I am. I would never hurt a woman—

never hurt anyone. It just happened. It was a terrible accident."

It's true. I believe him. I know and trust him, despite our circumstances. No matter what my husband has done, he's not someone who would purposefully hurt anyone. He's one of the kindest men I know. The most patient. Soft-spoken. Loving.

I can't make sense of this.

"So, tell the police that. Tell them the truth. They don't have any reason not to trust you."

He shifts in place, and I catch a whiff of the sweat on his skin—metallic and feral. Wild. He's a caged animal, trapped by his own horrible mistakes. "You haven't seen her."

"We'll just talk to her, then. You can tell her I know about you two and that you're sorry, that we'll pay for her medical care... I mean, the home insurance will cover that, right? If she was hurt here?" We certainly don't have that kind of money in our accounts. We're still making payments from the time James was hospitalized with pneumonia.

His hands come to rest on my upper arms. "You aren't listening to me. She won't care about that. She's going to tell the police I attacked her. If we let her go, I will go to jail."

I swallow, staring into those sea-blue eyes. The same eyes that brimmed with tears when I walked down the aisle, the eyes I held on to as I brought our children into the world, the eyes that have brought me so much comfort, safety, and peace over the decade we've been together. Now, something deep inside them is nearly unrecognizable.

"What do you want to do, then?" I ask breathlessly. "Give me our options."

He shakes his head, releasing my arms and stepping

back. When he speaks again, our future flashes in front of my eyes—empty and broken. As if we're as dead as the woman in the basement soon will be if we don't help her.

This will be our downfall.

He drags a finger and thumb over his nose, then cups his cheek, releasing a puff of air through his lips. "Honestly, I don't see that we have any."

CHAPTER THREE

ANDI

Spencer pushes open the door to the basement and flips on the light. It doesn't make a huge difference, honestly. The single bulb in the center of the room below is dim and still flickers on occasion. It's just enough light to see your way down the stairs. Once there, plastic storage bins are stacked into mountains across the room, casting shadows in every direction.

We shouldn't go down there.

I don't want to see this. Her. I'll never be able to unsee it. I know this, and yet, I find myself following Spencer down each step as if I don't know what's waiting for us at the bottom.

As if we could ever come back from this.

Will we? Do I want us to? To be honest, I'm not sure. All I know is that I can't allow myself to think about what he's done, how he's betrayed me, until I deal with this.

This is an emergency, and as much as I'm hurting, I need

to focus on one thing at a time. Or else my sadness will open up and swallow me whole.

I can feel it now, the grief, the stress, the anger, radiating like waves of heat against my skin. Waiting to strike. Waiting to remind me Spencer cheated. He lied. He betrayed me.

I pulse my fists. That doesn't matter right now. It can't.

The room smells damp and musty, like earth and dust, its air several degrees cooler than the rest of the house. Under my palm, the handrail is rough, coated in several layers of poorly applied paint, much like the door. You have to be careful of the underside of the rail, which has given me splinters on multiple occasions.

The steps are wooden, each one just two thin boards lying side by side, with the slightest crack between them. Between each step, you can see down into the shadows. If your foot slipped through, it's easy to imagine it could be swallowed up by the darkness of it all.

Nearing the bottom, I expect to hear her whimpering—screaming, maybe—begging for help, begging us not to hurt her, but I hear nothing. I don't look up until my feet hit the concrete floor. Spencer is just in front of me. I could use his body to shield me from having to see this if I wanted, but instead, I take it all in.

The woman sits on the floor in the center of the room, her back against one of the four thick wooden posts that stand in a solid line down the room. There is a rectangle of gray tape over her mouth.

He tied her up.

He taped her mouth.

He's holding her prisoner.

Bile rises in my throat as I appraise our surroundings,

deciding my next move. My dizzy thoughts warn me that I may pass out.

Beneath the tape, I notice her chin quivering. Is it from fear or pain? Rage, maybe?

This isn't okay.

How could he do this?

She jerks against whatever is binding her hands, scorching him with a vengeful stare. Spencer has moved things back, so there's a clear circle around her, though I spy an old pool stick lying on the ground, just out of her reach. I suspect that was the source of the sound I heard earlier.

If she stretched her foot out just a bit, she could graze where it was likely standing minutes ago. Clearly, she knocked it too far in the wrong direction. It's no use to her where it lies now. Still, Spencer crosses the distance between them and kicks the pool stick farther away.

Can't be too careful. I can almost hear him thinking it.

Beautiful despite the blood caked into her dark-blonde hair, she pins me with a defiant glare. If I expected her to be cowering or begging for help, it's obvious now that won't happen.

She is furious, not terrified.

I study her, then him, then him watching her. How is this real? How is any of this real?

"I didn't want this," he says finally, breaking the silence. It's unclear which one of us he's talking to, but her head turns slightly to look at him.

"Spencer…" I whisper his name. When neither of them looks at me, I realize I'm not sure I even said it aloud. We can't do this. We have to let her go. We aren't these people.

I should say one of these things—*any* of these things—but I can't find my voice. Is this really what he's capable of?

The affair is hard enough to swallow, but this? This is the work of a monster.

I'm unable to converge the two images of my husband now floating through my mind—the man who's endlessly patient and kind, who never raises his voice at me or the kids, and now this...this man who has a woman tied up in our basement.

How can they be the same person?

They can't.

Which is why this all must be a dream.

"I didn't," he goes on. "I don't. But you've given me no choice. I can't let you out now. You've made it clear you'll go to the police."

I wait for her to deny it, to assure him she won't—even through the tape—but instead, it almost looks like she's smiling. The edges of the tape curl up with her cheeks, wrinkling the same as the skin around her eyes.

"Just tell him you won't go to the police," I whisper. I hate her as much as I want to save her, but I won't let her ruin my life. That's exactly what this will do. If I let Spencer go through with this, we'll both go to jail. It's better to take our chances with the police, isn't it? Better to tell them the truth and let them work it out. Surely he realizes that. "Promise him you won't. It was an accident. We all know he didn't mean for this to happen." I say it, though in all reality, we both know I have no idea if it's true. Only Spencer's word.

Aside from small, white lies, I thought he'd never tried to deceive me, but now...

Now, I find myself praying he's telling the truth.

Praying this is *just* an affair.

An accident.

Anything but what it looks like.

With a swift shake of her head, she adjusts herself slowly, obviously stiff and sore. I catch a glimpse of a set of metal handcuffs around her wrists—ones I suspect he got out of my bedroom drawer—and wince.

I can't believe he put them on her.

Those were mine.

Ours.

To my horror, I notice how swollen her wrist appears. "You put handcuffs on her. Didn't you say her wrist is broken?" I move around to the back of the post to get a better look. Spencer follows closely behind.

"Yeah, it looks like it, but I had no other way to get her to stay put. She was fighting—"

"Jesus, Spencer, look!" I gesture toward the way her wrist has swollen, purpling, splotchy skin protruding out over the hard, metal edges of the silver handcuffs. *He made them so tight.* Disgust bubbles in my belly. "This is inhumane. She needs to see a doctor. Where is the key? Come on." I reach for the handcuffs, and when I take hold of them, she cries out in pure agony. "I'm so sorry." Even muffled under the tape, the sound is enough to send a sharp pain through my chest. This isn't right. We can't do this.

Spencer remains still, staring at me with unyielding determination. "If you take off her handcuffs, *she will run.*" He says the final three words slowly as if I might not understand. "She will knock things over, free her mouth, and scream so loud the neighbors will hear it." He looks down, then shakes his head. "I'm sorry, honey, but no. I can't risk it."

"No? What the hell do you mean *no*?"

"I can't give you the keys. She has to stay handcuffed. For both of our sakes."

"What are you talking about? Can't you see it's cutting off her circulation? There has to be another way."

His lips downturn. "I'm sorry, but no."

I squeeze my eyes shut, resisting the urge to throttle him. I understand he's in shock right now, that he's scared, but he has to see this is wrong. "Please, let's tie her arms instead. Or tape them like her mouth. We'll do it up higher, where it won't have to hurt her so badly."

He seems to contemplate it, then sighs. "Okay. Fine. Good idea." He moves across the room, grabbing a roll of tape from where he'd left it on a stack of storage bins filled with Christmas decorations. I watch as he tears a long piece off with his teeth and approaches her again.

He passes the tape to me and squats down, then wraps his arms around her from the side and tugs her backward hard against the post with a groan. I wince, squeezing my eyes closed. This all feels like a nightmare I can't wake up from.

Please. Please wake up.

He connects her arms near her elbows, despite her cries of protest.

"We're only trying to help," I whisper. It's a lie. We're hurting her worse. I can see it on her face, hear it in her wails.

Spencer secures her arms together with several pieces of tape, running his hands along the seam over and over again.

Once he's sure it's secure, he reaches into his pocket and pulls out the key to the handcuffs, clicking it into the small lock.

With a quick turn, the cuffs pop open. One side clatters to the floor, but the side on her swollen wrist stays put, held in place by skin. I reach forward, easing it off. Her cries turn to moans.

"I'm sorry," I whisper as I give a final tug, freeing her wrist at once. Her hands drop to the ground, slamming into the concrete, and she screams again.

"Sorry, sorry." I wince, baring my teeth. I should've thought to catch them, easing them down, but honestly, my head is swimming with so many thoughts right now I'm struggling to make sense of anything.

She whimpers as her sobs taper off. The impression the cuff left on her swollen wrist is terrible, a deep indentation in swollen, bruising skin.

"It's going to be okay," I whisper. I'm not sure if I'm telling her or myself.

Either way, it feels wrong. It sits heavy on my tongue, the weight of the lie too gargantuan to swallow.

It's never going to be okay again, and every single person in the room seems to know it.

CHAPTER FOUR

ANDI

Back upstairs, I scrub my hands in the kitchen sink, trying to quiet my racing thoughts.

Finally, I have an explanation for what I've felt since I walked into the house. Something *is* wrong. Something about the air *is* off.

Now, I know.

I wish I didn't. Better to be ignorant than complicit.

"I know what you must think of me." His voice behind me is low, filled with regret and anguish.

I swat the faucet, flicking the water off and spinning around to grab a towel. "Do you? Well, please tell me, Spence, because to be honest, I have no idea what to think of you."

His head perks up, eyes wild. "It was an accident. I never meant—"

"Which part? The sex? Or just the part where you tied her up in our basement?" I toss the towel on the counter, jabbing my fists into my hips.

His gaze falls to the floor again. "I... I made a mistake, Andi. I never should've slept with her. I never should've let the affair continue. It was a stupid mistake. One I'll regret for the rest of my life. I never wanted to hurt you."

"Well, too late for that." Betraying tears sting my eyes, and I look away. I'm so angry with him. So, so angry, but if I let myself go down that rabbit hole, I'm not sure I'll ever make it back out.

No, we have to focus on one problem at a time. Even if it kills me.

"I should've just let her tell you the truth. Then none of this would be happening. I was so scared I'd lose you if you knew about the affair." Tears well in his own eyes then, his head falling forward. "Now I'm going to lose you anyway."

"Don't do that," I snap, jabbing a finger at him. "Don't act like you're the victim here. Don't try to make me feel sorry for you. You're the one who cheated, Spencer. I would've never cheated on you!" My voice cracks, and I pause. I can't afford to break down right now. "No one held a knife to your throat and forced you into her bed. No one forced you. *You* cheated. *You* lied. And you just kept doing it. You'd probably still be doing it if this hadn't happened, wouldn't you?"

He doesn't answer straight away, and I can't bear to look at him any longer. I've tried so hard to be everything he needed. And in the end, it still wasn't enough. *I* still wasn't enough. Maybe that's what stings the most in situations like this, feeling like you're not enough for the person who is your whole world.

I blink back tears. "You're the reason we're in this mess.

Now you need to tell me how we're going to get out of it. What was your plan before I got here?"

He clears his throat, resting a hand on the counter. "Well, I was just taking it one second at a time, to be honest."

"Meaning what?" I feel like I'm losing my mind. Why does he seem so calm about all of this? Why isn't he as terrified as I am?

"Meaning I have no idea what my next move was going to be. When I saw her at the bottom of the stairs, when I realized what it would look like... I just panicked. I knew I needed her to be gone before the kids got home."

The kids. *Shoot.* I hadn't even thought to worry about them... I check my watch. "We've got about two hours until that happens. That's not enough time for us to make any sort of decision about how to handle this. I'll have to... I'll have to take them away for the night. Or for the weekend, maybe?" I'm thinking out loud at this point. "What do you think? How long will you need?"

How long will he need to do what? I'm not sure I know. I'm not sure I want to know.

His face is pale when he answers. "You're going to leave me alone?"

"Spence, we can't bring our kids into this house with her down there. It's not safe for them. Not to mention...if they were to hear something. See something." I shudder at the thought. "They can't be here. Please. You have to see that."

"No, I get that, but..."

"But what? You were handling this alone before."

He's shaking as he nods, visibly trying to appear calmer than he does. I hate this. I hate the way I'm talking to him— hate myself for caring. He's the one who cheated, who broke our vows, broke my heart... I shouldn't care, but that doesn't change the fact that I do. *What is wrong with me?*

"What other options are there? I can't have them here. You're not in a state to see them right now." I think of tiny James and sweet Ava uncovering the horror I just discovered. They'd never recover. Never forgive us. They'll need years of therapy to get over what their father has done if I can't protect them from it.

Another image flashes through my mind—a Netflix special, our kids' faces plastered across the front as they reveal the dark secret their father kept hidden in the basement.

They're on a stage recounting their story...

James had just gone down into the basement for a stray ball when he discovered her that day.

Now, they're in their thirties, unmarried, unemployed. Agoraphobics. Neither of them can hold down any sort of job or commit to anyone because of their childhood.

It's all our fault...

I shake the thoughts away. No. I won't let that happen. I refuse.

"We have to protect them from this, Spencer. They'll never survive it. This will ruin them." Has it ruined us? No. I can't think about that. I can't make any decisions yet. About him. About our marriage. There are more pressing matters at hand. One thing at a time.

"No, you're right." He swipes a hand through his hair. "I'll...I'll figure something out. You shouldn't have to help me with...whatever I decide."

"Okay, good." To try to tamp down the guilt I feel, I busy myself straightening things on the counter, turning the paper towels until they're not too loose on the roll, adjusting the salt and pepper shakers so you can easily read the S and P.

I'm not sure what I'm doing, but anything feels better than nothing. I need to control something when everything feels wholly out of control.

Why should I feel guilty for letting him clean up his own mess? I had nothing to do with this. I want nothing to do with this...

And yet...

I love him.

The whisper of truth in my mind can't be tidied. It can't be quieted. I love him. I want to protect him.

When I turn back toward him, he's still standing there, staring into space with that pitiful expression on his features.

"Spencer."

He looks up as if he'd forgotten I'm standing here.

"What are you going to do?" I tap my finger on the island countertop nervously as I ask the question. "Please... Please think. You need a plan."

I need him to save us. Need him to make this all okay again.

His face wrinkles, something breaking inside the both of us as he says his next words. "I am not a killer."

"I know you aren't." I move across the room, pulling him into a hug. It's the most natural thing in the world—holding him, loving him. Wanting to make it all better. Just like with the kids. In the end, we all become something like mothers to our own husbands, don't we? Finding things, fixing things, mending this, fetching that.

The impulsive need I feel to make his problems go away is insatiable.

But there is nothing to find. Nothing to mend. Nothing I can do to fix this. I wish more than anything we could go back to a day ago, a few hours ago even, when none of this had happened.

If we could just rewind this, take it all back...

We're good people. Normal, honest people.

These things don't happen to people like us.

"What am I going to do?" he cries, his chin resting on my shoulder. "I can't just let her go. I can't let her go to the police and make me into some monster. I'm not a monster. You know I'm not. I can't go to jail. I just can't."

"No one's going to jail," I say, hugging him tighter and rubbing his back. It's the way I've comforted the kids over a lost toy or dying pet. Only this problem can't be solved through a late-night run to the toy store or a replacement goldfish. This is big. Dangerous. It could be the end of everything, and I'm still not sure that has set in all the way for either of us.

Whatever we decide, we'll never be the people we were yesterday.

"We'll figure this out. There has to be a way to talk to her, to explain, or to...even to discredit her somehow. I could be your alibi. I could say you were with me. That we weren't near her. It'll be our word against hers. Or...or maybe you could say she broke into the house and—"

"The text messages." His words shut me up as he pulls back. "Even if I delete them from both of our phones, I think the police could recover them. They'll see I invited her here, and then it'll look even worse because we lied."

"Okay. You're right. Okay." I pace the room, trying to

think. "Does she have anyone who'll be looking for her? Anyone who knows she's here?"

He shakes his head. "No, I don't think so. She isn't married, and most of her friends are industry people. Not ones she keeps closely in touch with. And she didn't tell anyone about us."

"You're sure? You trust her?"

"Before today? Yeah, I did. She didn't tell anyone, Andi. It was a risk for her, too. There was a chance she could get dropped from the agency if anyone found out. With all the stuff going on, the MeToo movement and all of that, relationships within the company—agents and clients—it's...well, it's highly frowned upon at a minimum."

"She's not your client, though. Is she Linda's? I don't remember you ever mentioning her."

"No, she's an actress." It's self-explanatory. Spencer's boss only works with musicians. "She's with Sarah. But it could still cause problems. There was a memo that went out a while back when it came out about Evan's affair with a client, and they made it clear. No tolerance. He was fired and she was dropped. Stewart had a meeting with corporate over it and everything. It was a huge deal. She wouldn't risk it for either of us." He pauses, his expression changing.

"What is it?"

"I just thought of something... I need to pull up her file, see what projects she's supposed to be working on right now. She was just supposed to be in town for the day. When she doesn't show up to set, her manager and agent will be notified. People will start to ask questions if they can't get in touch with her."

Panic spreads in my chest, spindly fingers wrapping

around my lungs, making it hard to breathe. "Well, check it then."

He pulls out his phone but hesitates. "They'll be able to see it. In the system. They'll know I pulled up her file."

"What choice do we have? Can't you just say you were looking at it for work?"

"Maybe." I can tell he's not convinced. "But it's risky. If we give anyone any reason to look into me, if they find the texts between us..."

"Okay, well, then we have to give another reason for why she won't show up." I pause, thinking. "Okay, how about this? She's flighty, right? An actress. They disappear all the time. Off to Cabo or Bora Bora or wherever." I wave my hand as if they're all the capricious stereotype I'm describing. "Can't we just make it look like she went somewhere?"

He presses his fingers to his temples, massaging them in slow circles with his eyes squeezed shut. "She's not exactly a celebrity, Andi. It's not like she has a private jet. She's a struggling actress who's had, like, I don't know, maybe a dozen minor roles. There would be records of it if she left the country. She'd have to get a plane ticket. It will be easy enough for the police to prove that didn't happen."

The police.

Every time he says the words, my insides clench.

A light bulb goes off in my mind. "But...that's even better, isn't it? It would look as if she's trying to appear fancier and more well-connected than she is. What screams social media more than that? We could post on her accounts, send an email to her manager and agent, and say she's taking a mental health break and needs some time away to...to reflect or disconnect or something. Either way, it points people away from us, it explains why she isn't going to be showing up to work, and if anyone looks into it too much, it'll just seem like she actually went on a road trip or something because she couldn't afford the international trip she's pretending to take."

I can see he's considering it, so I add, "It would at least buy us time to work out a better plan. For now, we just have to do something. And it prevents you from having to open her file and point anyone's eyes or attention in our direction."

"Alright. It's not a bad plan." He moves around the island and pulls open a drawer, revealing a small, silver clutch from inside it. He retrieves a phone from the drawer —*her* phone, I realize—and lays it on the counter. "I can send the email from her phone, but I shouldn't do it from here. Police can track that, can't they? Locations and stuff. It's too late to make it look like she was never here, but we could make it look like she's left. I could take her phone and go to the airport or a car rental place."

"The park," I say quickly. "The airport is too risky if anyone does actually look into this. They'd be able to see she never purchased a ticket and that would look strange. And a car rental place will definitely have security cameras. Drive to Centennial Park, send the message, and turn off her phone. Then take it somewhere else and throw it out. Oh, and leave *your* phone here, so it looks like you never left the house if they were to track it."

"What about the texts?"

"Delete them before you turn off her phone. Actually, you should factory reset her phone, just to be safe." My blood runs cold. "I'm not sure if that's enough, Spencer. I'm honestly not. But it's something. Right now, we just need to do *something*. If we wait too long, we risk being caught even more. We have to give people a reason to stop asking about her for a while. Until we can figure everything else out."

He gives a single, sharp jerk of his head. "Right. Okay. You're not coming with me?"

"Someone should stay here with her, don't you think? Just in case she tries to break out or starts screaming or something." It seems like the most logical plan, but I can tell he doesn't agree. "I'm not going to let her go, if that's what you're worried about."

His voice falters. "It's just... If you do, that's it for me, you know? I'm done. My life, effectively, is over. And what if she hurts you?"

"I'm not going to let her out. I won't even go down there."

"Promise?"

I drag a finger over my heart in the shape of an X. "Promise. Now go. We're running out of time."

He takes a step away from the island, picking up her clutch and phone as he does, and walks backward toward the living room. He tucks the items under his shirt with a sheepish look and points toward the front door. "Cameras."

"Right."

Finally, he turns and leaves. I stay frozen in place as I listen to the car start up, then back out of the driveway.

Once he's gone, I puff out a long, slow breath of air, trying to keep from crying. If hopelessness sets in, I'm going to lose it. I have to keep busy, keep planning, keep moving.

I grab my phone from the counter and swipe my thumb up the screen to unlock it. His mention of our doorbell cameras reminded me I should check them. I'm hoping to search through the footage of her arrival and delete it.

I tell myself I don't need to go through the torture of watching them together. Did she kiss him hello? Did he take her in his arms and say how much he'd missed her?

Either way, I can't leave it in our cloud should the police come around asking questions.

But, it turns out, I'm in luck. Instead of a live camera view, I find only a black screen. Our camera battery is dead. The last recording is from three days ago.

Perfect.

I place the phone down. At least that means there's no evidence she arrived in the first place, but a small, demented part of me knows I wanted to see them together.

I wanted to see it with my own eyes, the proof of what he's telling me.

Still, I can't help feeling relieved at what is a small saving grace. There will be no video footage to prove she arrived here. None of our neighbors' houses face us at the right angle for their cameras to see our front door or driveway. We found that out when a few of our packages went missing once before.

My eyes flick to the basement door—decision made—and I cross the room and push it open, staring down into the darkness.

Sorry, babe. Looks like we're both guilty of breaking promises now.

CHAPTER FIVE

SPENCER

S hit.
    Shit. Shit. Shit. Shit.
Shit.

I've really done it this time—and there's no going back.
The moment in the garage when I heard footsteps coming
from inside the house, my heart rattled in my chest so loudly
I was sure I was going to pass out. I just knew Heidi had
managed to escape and was roaming the house looking for
me, looking for her phone, calling the police, coming for
revenge.

I dropped my tools and grabbed a towel from the small
stack of ones I use to clean the cars. Suffocation isn't ideal, I
hate the idea of having to look her in the eyes when I do it,
but if that was what it came down to, I wanted to be
prepared.

I never in my wildest dreams imagined it would be my
wife waiting inside for me. When I saw her standing outside
the basement door, I'm fairly certain my life flashed before

my eyes in a very real, very *this is the end of everything* sort of way.

Their differences are stark—the blonde hair is where the similarities end. Heidi is long and lean, always tan, always glowing. With legs that seem unending and a body that showcases the hours she puts in at the gym. She's toned. Strong. She looks like who she is—an actress, a model, a star. While Cassandra—Andi, as I've always called her—is softer. Both in temperament and body type. Softer even still, now that we've had the kids. She's never concerned herself with her appearance, aside from getting occasional highlights, and she doesn't bother getting her nails done or dressing up all that often. Her focus is on our kids and on her students at school. On me.

I realize what an ass I sound like, for the record. And I'm not complaining. I love my wife. She's beautiful—sexy, even. She makes me laugh. Takes care of me. Takes care of the house. The kids. She's kind, and she obsesses over making people feel welcome and loved.

Do you think I was rude to Ava's new dance teacher earlier?

No, why?

I can't stop thinking that I didn't say enough when Ms. Kaiti asked if we'd met her.

You said yes we had.

Yes, but should I have added something else? Should I have said we're so glad she's here? Or that Ava loves it there? I feel like I was short with her, and I didn't mean to be.

I'm sure she didn't think anything of it.

These are the conversations I have with her regularly.

Worried about offending someone by...*not greeting them enough?*

Or not saying hello to the neighbors when we see them outside. Not asking Mrs. Grady how her mother is feeling when we pass her in the grocery store—*you know she's been sick.*

It's constant and never ending, and she truly feels the anxieties she expresses. They worry her. Keep her awake at night.

Which is why, when I walked around the corner and saw her standing there, I knew I had to tell her something, had to tell her about Heidi and that Heidi was now locked in our basement. I felt both relief—knowing she'd be able to make this better somehow since she always did—and utter terror.

There's no way she's going to let me go through with this.

To ask Andi to kill someone—to stand back and allow me to kill someone, even—is like asking a dog to breathe under-water. It's not just that she won't *want* to, she physically, emotionally, spiritually, and mentally won't be able to.

Which is why I said...this is the end of everything.

It's not like I want to do it. I don't want to hurt anyone, and certainly not Heidi. What Andi doesn't know, what I'd prefer for her not to know, is that Heidi and I knew each other long before she was a client of the agency.

In what feels like another life, we grew up together. Went to high school together. We weren't friends, per se, but we ran around in the same crowds. A few years older than I was, I'd often see her at the parties I was attending, then try and fail to work up the courage to talk to her.

Even back then, she was a knockout. Always popular, almost...effervescent. It seemed like no one could get close to her. She was untouchable. Even her dearest friends didn't seem to know who she was.

It didn't shock anyone when she left school her senior year to pursue acting seriously. She started in Nashville and Atlanta—back before Atlanta had the film scene it has today —but it wasn't long before we heard she was out in L.A. rubbing elbows with the rich and famous.

After that, New York.

Chicago.

Back to L.A.

Back to New York.

She did a few commercials, some print modeling, but for whatever reason, directors and casting agents weren't seeing her as a leading lady. First, it was her Southern accent, which she worked hard to shed. Then, it was that she looked too young. Too innocent. She made adjustments accordingly. No matter what she did, it never seemed to be enough.

She wasn't giving up though, and eventually, several years in, she landed her first role in a feature film.

Since then, there have been other roles—characters with actual credited names—both on TV and film. She's changed. Living in New York and L.A., and being part of an industry that treats plastic surgery and cosmetic procedures like hair-cuts, will do that to you. When I saw her again for the first time, I hardly recognized her. Even still, when I look hard enough, I can see the girl I knew back then.

So, no. I don't want to hurt her. I certainly don't want to kill her.

I'm not a killer.

I've never in my life hurt another human being—there were no fights in school, and I don't spank the children as a means of discipline. It's not something I take any sort of pleasure in, and certainly not something I take lightly.

Still, the moment she said she was going to tell Andi, something primal was awakened in me. I had to stop her. Had to protect my family.

What I told Andi was true: I didn't mean for her to hit her head on the edge of the island, didn't mean for her to fall down the basement stairs and get hurt, but once it happened, I panicked. What else could I do?

I remember thinking she was dead at first as I looked down the stairs at where she'd fallen. Her wrist was bent at an odd angle, her face flat on the concrete next to the bottom steps, blonde hair splayed all around.

But then she groaned.

I breathed for the first time in what felt like a lifetime.

The rest is a blur. I don't remember getting the handcuffs from the drawer in Andi's nightstand, don't remember cuffing her. Don't remember what I said to her—if I said anything.

I came upstairs, cleaned the blood from the island and kitchen floor, then went back down with a glass of water. She wouldn't drink it. I couldn't blame her, but it wasn't poisoned. I drank it myself, staring at her, assessing the injuries.

Then, I began to beg.

This wasn't what I intended. I don't know why I handcuffed you. Are you alright? I'm happy to let you go, but you have to promise me you won't go to Andi.

Andi? No, she was going to the police, she'd said, her teeth coated with blood.

I knew she was being honest, though I don't know why. If she'd lied, maybe I really would've let her go.

Then again, maybe not.

I retreated to the garage with a fuzzy sort of single-mindedness. I wasn't sure what I was looking for—a weapon of some sort. She needed to go away. I needed to get rid of her, to clean her up as if she were a spilled drink on the kitchen floor. Andi and the kids would be home in just a few hours, and she couldn't be there.

Now, with my wife home and plans interrupted, I'm not sure how I'll ever convince Andi that plan is still our only choice.

It takes a full thirty minutes to get to Centennial Park, the same park where we've taken the kids to play on Saturdays when the entire lawn fills with food trucks and live music, the park where Andi and I celebrated our first and second anniversaries with an evening picnic.

I stare at the people walking past—couples, families, businessmen on important calls. Each of them is blissfully unaware of me. Of the bitter cracking sound as my world splinters before my very eyes.

I lift Heidi's phone, staring down at the screen. It's a picture of her reflection in a hair and makeup chair, bright light bulbs glowing around the frame of the mirror.

She looks happy—like she has the world at her feet. I guess she always did.

Maybe it won't be the worst thing if the police find our texts or the phone call between us as we decided where to meet. If I'm right, they will also be able to see that she left our house before coming here. That she was safe, sound, and alive when we last saw her pulling out of our driveway.

If I'm wrong, well, I think we've already established how completely fucked we are in that case.

I type in her password—the four digits I watched her type just hours ago, before she told me the reason she was there. She'd shown me screenshots of our texts and photos—proof of the affair. She said she was going to send the screenshots and photos to Andi—all the proof she needed. She said she was going to ruin my life.

I had no choice.

I open up one of her social media accounts first and scroll through her posts, trying to get a feel for her voice. Andi would be so much better at this than me. Finally, when I feel as ready as I'll ever be, I tap out a message, rereading it several times.

I keep it short, simple.

I'm going through some very personal things right now, so I'll be off all the socials for a while. Much-needed mental health break, here I come. #SorryNotSorry #OneWayTickettoFiji #MentalHealthisImportant #SelfCare

I know from her previous posts she uses a lot of hashtags, though I've never been one to care about or appreciate them, so I hope I've done it well. At the last minute, I add two emojis before the hashtags—the sun and an island—and consider calling Andi to ask for her approval.

In the end, I decide against it. I can do this. Just like we talked about.

I press the button to make the post go live.

Then I copy and paste the same message onto her two other social media accounts. Next, I open her email account and read through a few she's recently sent. I want to see how she speaks here, too. If it's different than on social media.

I notice a few patterns right away—she never includes a greeting and always signs off *Yours, Heidi*.

Feeling as prepared as I can be, I send an email to her manager, Evelyn, and agent, Sarah. I don't know Sarah well, but I know her enough to understand she's great at her job. If this email, carrying with it the news that her client is stepping away for a while, costs her money, she'll be furious. She'll do whatever it takes to get her back to set. I just have to hope our plan is enough to fool her.

Sorry to do this over email, but I've just received some really bad news. Family health stuff. I'm okay, but I need to take a step back and try to deal with it. I'm going to be unreachable for a while, turning off the phone and disconnecting while I put all my focus into this. Please cancel all projects for the foreseeable future. I'll let you know when I feel ready to come back. I'm so sorry again.
Yours,
Heidi

With that taken care of, I factory reset her phone—*am I sure I want to delete all content and settings? Yes*—and turn it off, then reach over into the passenger side floorboard, feeling for the brown paper bag from my take-out lunch. I've seen enough episodes of SVU to know that if anyone sees a phone and purse lying in a public trash can, they'll likely report it to the police. I need to hide it. When I locate the bag, I quickly remove the receipt. Maybe I'm being paranoid at this point, but I want to be sure there's nothing that can be traced back to me. Could they look at the time stamp from the receipt and pull camera footage to find out who I am? It's too risky.

With the receipt safely crumpled in my cup holder, I stuff her small purse and phone inside the bag, rolling the top down as low as it will go.

I eye the trash can up ahead of the car, knowing once I throw this out, our fate is sealed. Decision made.

Heidi Dawson will never set foot outside of our basement.

I reach for the door handle, easing the door open before immediately pulling it closed.

Shit.

Up ahead, there's a police officer walking in my direction. He's distracted with his lunch, a large sandwich wrapped in yellow paper, but I can't risk it.

I have to leave.

Have to get out of here.

I'll get rid of her things soon enough. For now, the most important thing is taken care of. I place the bag down on the floorboard and back out of my parking space, hands trembling on the wheel.

I don't check to see if the police officer ever looks my way, but still, I feel as if I'm being watched.

CHAPTER SIX

ANDI

She watches me without a sound as I near the bottom of the steps. I don't know what to say to her. There are things I want to know, things I want to ask, but they're inappropriate right now.

I'm not delusional enough to think otherwise. Still, it's impossible to stop comparing the two of us. Our differences.

Is that why he chose her? Someone so unlike me?

She's blonde, like I am, like his ex before me, Stephanie.

Spencer has always liked blondes.

But our similarities end there.

She's beautiful; I'm plain.

She's rail thin and tall; I'm far from either.

I look as old as I am, thirty-five last month, a year younger than Spencer, and Heidi looks much younger than either of us. Even beneath the dried blood on her face, she radiates with smooth, inexpressive skin that tells me she paid a fortune for that sort of agelessness.

"I'm Andi," I tell her, keeping my distance. She doesn't try to say anything. "You're Heidi?"

She puffs out a breath through her nose, quiet for a moment. Eventually, she nods.

"You're...you're an actress?"

Again, she nods.

"We don't want to hurt you," I say gently, my voice cracking. "I know how scared you must be. I'm scared too, to be honest. I'm...I'm not a person who does this sort of thing. I'm a teacher. I make donations to animal shelters and carry around those little blessing bags for the homeless. Have you seen those? They're on social media. Bags you fill with socks and snacks and hand warmers..." I pause. Why am I rambling? She seems just as confused as I feel. "What I'm trying to say is I'm a good person. I'm so sorry he's done this to you. He isn't thinking. I can... I can help you. I want to find a way out of this for all of us, but you have to help me, too."

Her eyes flick to the stairs.

"He's a good man. You must've seen that...before." Squeezing my eyes shut, I force away the images that flash in my mind—images of the two of them together, his lips on hers, his hands on her body, clothing flying. If I think about it too long, I'll be sick. I pulse my fists. We have bigger problems than the affair right now. I must remember that. "Things just got out of hand."

It's partially her fault, anyway. If she hadn't been so determined to come forward about the affair—if she hadn't been sleeping with a married man in the first place—none of this would be happening.

It will be easier with her gone, I tell myself. With her out of the way, I don't have to worry about competing for my husband. But I want her far away, distracted, moved on, not *dead*.

"You don't have to go to the police about this. You must realize that you don't. He made a mistake. Obviously, things got heated and you...well, you fell, right? It was an accident. Do you really want to see him go to jail for that?"

Her stare is unyielding, her sea-green eyes filled with hatred.

"I don't think you do. Not if you care about him as much as I think you do. I know you must be angry with him. Trust me, I'm angry too. Furious. And he deserves our anger. But he doesn't deserve to go to prison. Our children don't deserve to lose him." I don't say the final part out loud: *I don't deserve to lose him.*

She scoffs from under the tape, rolling her eyes and looking away from me finally.

"I would take the tape off your mouth so we could talk, but I don't trust you not to scream. I can't have you screaming."

She makes no moves to convince me she won't.

"Come on, Heidi." Her name scalds my tongue.

I hate her.

I hate her.

I hate her.

"I'm trying to help you here. I don't have to do that. Another woman in my shoes might not. I could easily just leave you down here in the dark."

I take a breath, forcing myself to calm down. "Look, I know you're upset, and rightfully so. I don't blame you, but you can see now what a misunderstanding this is. I think you know he isn't this man. I think you know he doesn't want to hurt you."

I step forward, squatting down in front of her. Pressing my fingers to the floor in front of me to keep from toppling over, I plead with her, woman to woman. "We're all adults here, right? Obviously, none of this is okay. He shouldn't have handcuffed you. He should've helped you after you got hurt."

My eyes travel over the blood caked in her hair and on her forehead. "I'm so sorry he didn't. You have no idea how sorry I am. And I realize that all means nothing unless I help you now, which is exactly what I'm trying to do. But I can't let you ruin my family. I can't."

I press my lips together. Does she understand what I'm saying? Does she even care? Would I, in her position? "So, show me a path. Another option. Tell me what to do, and I'll do it. No one wants this to get any worse, you know? If you could just swear to us that you won't turn him in...we could fix it somehow. I really think we could. There has to be another way to deal with this besides getting the police involved."

She must not believe me, must think I'm trying to trick her.

"Can I get you something?" I offer, hoping to make her trust me. "The floor down here can't be comfortable. It's always so cold." I press my palm to the cool concrete. "I could bring you a blanket, maybe. Or two? One to sit on. I'm sure you'd like some pain medicine." I gesture to the gash on her forehead. "I know that can't feel too great."

She's quiet.

"Would you like that?"

Finally, she gives a curt nod. Proof of life. The first sign that she's at least hearing what I'm saying.

"Is there something specific you'd like to drink? We have water or tea...some wine...the kids have apple juice or grape juice." I list the options slowly, waiting for her to react. I know she can't answer by speaking, but a nod of her head would really help me out. We don't have to be monsters about this. We don't have to be uncivil. "I think that's all." When she gives no reaction, I start to go over the options again. "Would you like water or hot tea or..."

She nods her head when I say tea.

"Great. Tea. Okay. I'll be right back."

Upstairs, I fill the kettle and place it on the stove before pulling a tea bag out of the box resting near the refrigerator. I love teas—all flavors, herbal, caffeinated or non—it's how I start and end my day. Spencer has never understood the obsession, but it makes for an easy Christmas or birthday gift, so he's always happy to pick some up.

Once the water is heated, I pour her mug, fully aware of how ridiculous it is to be preparing tea for a woman we're currently holding captive in our basement, but it's all I know to do. I have to do something.

I check the time as I move down the hall. I have just over an hour before the kids will arrive home from school. Just over an hour to convince Heidi and Spencer that we can somehow make it out of this with no more bloodshed.

In the hallway, I open the linen closet—filled with spare blankets, pillowcases, towels, and other random junk we have no predetermined place for—and pull down two comforters I don't mind parting with, should it come to that.

Her body wrapped in the blankets. Blood spreading across the fabric.

No.

It won't come to that. I have to believe it won't.

At this point, I think I'm the only one who believes it.

I place the comforters on the counter in the kitchen and head to the bathroom to search for ibuprofen.

A few minutes later, with two pills in one hand, the comforters tucked under my arm, and the mug of tea in my other hand, I make my way back down the stairs.

When I arrive, I place the mug down out of her reach while it cools and attempt to spread the blanket out next to her.

Slowly, she eases herself onto it with a sort of scooting movement. I help out, pushing the blanket over with my foot —I don't dare lower my face that close to her legs or feet for fear she'll kick me. It's what I would do in her position.

Once she's on the blanket, I place the other one over her legs gently. "Here you go. It's not much, but it'll help." I open my hand. The one I'd been gripping the two small, rust-colored pills in now boasts four red circles in the center of my palm, one on either side of each pill where they've melted.

"I'm going to have to take your tape off," I warn her, preparing myself. If this goes badly, Spencer will never forgive me. "If you scream, I won't try to help you again."

Her eyes lock with mine, then flick back down to the pills. Finally, she tilts her chin forward ever so slightly.

Permission.

I ease forward, heart thudding in my chest, sweat gathering at my brows—even in the cold basement, I suddenly feel like I'm under a heat lamp—and reach for a corner of the gray tape.

With the first tug of the tape from her cheek, she winces. I offer an apologetic grimace. "I'm sorry. I know this must hurt." I ease it back farther, revealing her cheek, her lips, her chin. Everything is sticky with residue from the tape. Raw and red from the pain of its removal. When she sucks in a breath from her mouth, I catch sight of her teeth, caked with blood.

She fell hard.

The double entendre isn't lost on me.

Fell for my husband. Fell down the stairs.

Once the last corner of the tape has been torn from her mouth, I step back, taking in the full view of her face for the first time. Even with the red patch blooming around her lips and the blood caked on her forehead, she looks calm. But also angry.

Justified, I know, but it's not as if *I* did this to her. I'm only trying to help. I'm just as angry as she is.

I hold out my hand. "I'll have to put these in your mouth," I say, giving her a better view of them. "I can't untape your arms just yet."

It's as if she expected as much. She doesn't argue but instead presses her lips together, studying the pills in my hand.

"It's just ibuprofen. I promise I'm not going to hurt you."

"Then...let me go." Her voice is soft. Not what I expected. "You could just let me go." I can hear the dryness of her throat, practically feel it. She's hoarse. As if she hasn't had anything to drink in days rather than hours. For the first time, I see a hint of fear in her eyes. "We can't let him get away with this."

"Of course not. I don't... I'm not looking at it like he's getting away with anything. I want to help us all deal with this. And I'm sorry, but I can't let you go. Not yet, anyway. Not until we've had a chance to talk everything through."

"Everything?" She scoffs. Spots of color speckle her cheeks. "How can you be okay with this? Any of this?"

"I never said I was okay with it." I lower my hand, my jaw tight. "I'm far from okay with any of this."

"And yet, you'll stand by him. Help him even."

"He's my husband," I say firmly, rubbing my free hand over the back of my neck. "He made a mistake. Everyone makes mistakes. He doesn't want to hurt you."

"Ah, so you're *that* kind of woman."

I ball my hands into fists, already offended before she's had a chance to elaborate. The muscles in my chest grow tight, making it difficult to catch my breath. "What kind of woman?"

One side of her lips lifts in a wry smirk. "The *stand by her man* kind. The apologist." Finally, her eyes find mine again. "The kind who believes him no matter what he says, no matter how many times he lies."

"He's not...he's not lying." My voice falters. "He told me about the affair. He told me it was a mistake."

"A mistake is forgetting to get gas before you get too far out of town or not remembering your coat when it's cold." She bares her teeth, scowling. "This is not a mistake, Andi. He did not make a *mistake*. He knew what he was doing. Knew it was wrong. And now that he's been caught, now that you know and he might go to prison—*now* he's sorry.

Now he feels bad. Now it's a mistake." She turns away from me again, mumbling under her breath with a flat, vacant expression. "If anyone made a mistake here, it was me."

"Look, I don't know what happened or how it all went down, but I do know that Spencer is a loving husband. A great father. He cares about our children. Our family. He would never do anything to intentionally hurt us. Or anyone else, for that matter. I'm not saying any of this is right. I'm so angry with him for what he did—"

"The person you're describing is the version of himself he lets you see. Don't you get that? You see what he lets you. Your experience with him is not all-encompassing. His being nice to you doesn't negate what he's done, what you can now see with your own eyes. And what about the fact that he jeopardized his entire career over this? Your family's future? Your safety. Does that sound like a loving husband and great father to you?"

I open my mouth to respond, but no words come out. Spencer is all of those things—he loves us, he provides for us, he takes care of us. But he also caused all of this. He's the reason we're in this mess.

Focus. I have to focus.

I will deal with my feelings for my husband once Heidi is free. Once this is all over.

"I'm telling you," she says, "he's a monster. You can choose to believe it or don't, but at this point, that says more about you than it does him."

"It's not that simple!" I rake my hand through my hair. "You're right. I never expected my husband to be capable of this, but what are any of us capable of on our worst day? Today doesn't take away all the good he's done, either."

Her lips curl with a sour grin. "So you're staying with him?"

Suddenly, I'm nauseous. I can't seem to swallow. "I... I found out half an hour ago. How could I be expected to make that decision already?"

A muscle in her cheek twitches. "You're down here, not letting me go. Not calling the police. I'd say you already have."

"We're in the middle of a crisis. I haven't even had a moment to think about my marriage. I'm too busy trying to help you," I tell her firmly.

Her jaw drops open. "Then either let me go or give me the pills and get out of my face."

I swallow and glance down at my hand, the decision weighing on my mind. Then again, it's not really a decision. I'm not going to let her go, not yet, and we both know it.

I lift the pills to her mouth and drop them in, then pick up the mug of tea. Before I can offer it to her, she swallows. The pills are gone.

"You could've waited. Don't you want a drink?"

She shakes her head when I hold it out.

"It's not poisoned, for Christ's sake. It's just tea." I lift it to my own lips and take a sip.

She wets her lips with a fixed look of concentration. Finally, she opens her mouth.

I lower the mug to her. "Careful, it's hot. I'll go slow." Cautiously, I place it on her bottom lip, turning it up some. When a splash of the brown liquid touches her tongue, she winces but swallows, tilting her chin to get more. She pulls back with her mouth full, cheeks puffed.

"Everything o—"

I see it coming a millisecond before it does. She puckers her lips and spews the steaming-hot liquid into my face, my eyes.

"*Ah!*" I fall backward, crying out, trying to swipe the source of the burning from my skin. I pull my shirt away from my body, using it to wipe my eyes.

When the white-hot pain subsides, I stare at her with a small intake of breath. I rub my brows, the skin tender and sensitive. Next to me, the mug is shattered on the ground, hot, brown liquid creeping in every direction.

"Why would you do that?" I demand, blood roaring in my ears. I jerk the blanket off her legs as she swipes her mouth with her shoulder, using the fabric to clean up the tea as much as I can. My knees ache as I bend to gather the shattered ceramic pieces of the mug.

I toss them onto the blanket.

She doesn't say another word as I finish cleaning up her mess and pick up the roll of tape. I slap a long piece over her mouth without a care, pressing it down with unnecessary force.

She doesn't wince or whine.

We're at an impasse. Neither of us can show our pain, even as my skin throbs like a bad sunburn.

The sound of the car in the driveway warns me Spencer has made it home. Quickly, I gather the blanket up and head for the stairs.

At the top, I flip off the light.

CHAPTER SEVEN

ANDI

When I hear him come into the house, I drop the cool washcloth onto the comforter, grab the last few broken shards of the mug and toss them into the trash. I shut the cupboard door where we keep our trash can with a stiff, sideways glance at the doorway just as he appears. Before he gets too good of a look at me, I ball the comforter up and disappear into the laundry room. Just then, it registers he was carrying a bag of fast food.

I can't believe his nerve.

I toss the comforter and washcloth into the washing machine and step back into the hallway. "You...stopped for lunch? Really?"

He looks down at the sack, appearing lost, then shakes his head. "Oh. No. This was from the other day. I brought it inside to throw it away. What's wrong with you?"

My lips turn down at his question. "Do you really have to ask?"

"Right."

"Well?" I demand, walking back into the kitchen. I immediately turn so he doesn't yet get a good look at my face. The redness is fading, but my skin hasn't completely returned to normal yet. "How did it go?"

In my peripheral vision, I see him pinch his nose, sliding his thumb and forefinger down either side as he always does when he's stressed. "Fine, I think. I posted on her social media, then emailed her agent and manager saying she was going through some things and needed to take a break. So, I guess that takes care of it for the time being. How were things here?"

"Fine. She's been quiet. I..." I need to find a way to ease into the conversation, to warn him of what I've done. I look over at him finally. "I took a blanket down to her to...make her more comfortable."

He looks as ill as if I'd said I released her. "You went down there? I asked you not to. You promised you wouldn't!"

"I'm sorry. I had to. Just to give her the blanket. I can't stomach the thought that she's sitting down there on the cold, damp concrete. It's freezing and filthy. We don't have to be cruel to her. Keeping her down there is a means of survival until we figure out what to do. But we can at least make sure she's comfortable."

He crosses the room and opens the cupboard, lingering over the trash can. I wait for him to notice the broken pieces of the mug, to ask what happened. Instead, he sets the bag in the trash can, hardly looking inside. "Comfortable before we kill her? That's an odd concept, isn't it?"

The casual way he says it makes me feel dizzy. He's talking about her as if she were a video game character, not a real-life human.

He shuts the door and turns to face me, his tone serious. "You do understand that we're going to have to kill her, don't you? We can't let her leave."

"Maybe we don't have to," I say. "Maybe we could talk to her. She obviously loves you—"

"We weren't in love, Andi. It was physical. An attraction. What I thought was a mutual understanding. And a mistake. More than anything, it was a terrible, terrible mistake. I never wanted to hurt you. I'm so sorry I have. I will do whatever it takes to make it right."

Is that even possible? Could he ever make this right? I look down, pinching my lips together as the petrified thoughts come. *Please don't cry. Pull it together, Andi. There is no time for this. You have to be brave right now. Stronger than you feel.*

"She isn't the woman I thought she was," Spencer goes on. "I can't convince her not to go to the police. Not unless you want to get a divorce and force me to be with her or something. That might work." He's joking. At a time like this? What is wrong with him? His eyebrows furrow, then release as he steps forward, holding out his hand to grip my chin. "What happened to your face? It's red."

"Nothing. I washed it." I swat him away. "And no, of course I don't want to divorce you. If I wanted to divorce you, if I didn't care about you, I would've already freed her. Would've let the cops come for you. I'm not, though. I'm trying to save you both."

It's a fool's errand. I should let them work out their own problems—let them both suffer for what they've done to me, to my kids, but deep down I know, even if I wanted to, I couldn't.

I love Spencer.

And sometimes, love is enough to make you do anything.

I check the time again. "Okay. We need to figure out what we're going to do about the kids. At this point, no matter what we do, they're going to be home before we've... gotten her out of there." *Dead or alive*, I think.

He seems to understand what I mean without saying the horrible words aloud.

"Can we call your parents?" he asks. "Could they watch them for a night or two?"

"They're out of town, remember? Dad is at a conference for work in Salt Lake City. Mom went with him." I pat my hand on the island, thinking.

"What about Jo?"

My fingers trace over the swirls in the granite pattern. "Um, I don't know. I haven't talked to her today. I think she mentioned her niece's birthday party this weekend, but I can't remember which day she said."

"Well, can you call and ask her to keep them? To buy us more time? Surely she can take them to the party with her. They'll behave."

"Yeah, I'm sure she would." I lift my phone from the countertop, trying to think of an excuse to give her. Spencer and I never ask anyone to keep the kids unless we have no other choice. We never want to be a burden. Maybe that's why we're in this mess. Maybe if I'd insisted on more alone time. If I'd prioritized our marriage...

No.

This is not that. Our marriage is fine. Spencer made a mistake because he did. It's not my failure that caused it.

"I'm going to tell her you're sick."

"Fine."

I find my best friend's name in my call log and click on it. It rings so long I'm sure she's not going to answer, but eventually, she does.

"Hey, what's up?"

"Hey. I need a favor."

"Well, it may cost you." She laughs, her voice warm. It makes me crave normalcy. It also makes me feel like I'll never laugh again. How can she not know my world is falling apart? How can she not sense it? I took advantage of the days when our biggest worry was what to cook for dinner and when we needed to take the cars to get the oil changed. If we get through this, I'll never make that mistake again. "What do you need?"

"Are you doing anything this weekend?"

"Lily's party is Sunday afternoon, but other than that, I don't think I have anything going on. What did you have in mind?"

"I was going to ask if you would keep the kids for me." I hate asking. Really, I do. Jo's great with the kids and they love her, but she's single again and carefree. I hate to bother her, but aside from my parents and Spencer's sister, who lives out of state, Jo is the only one I'd trust with them.

"Yeah, of course. When?" she says without missing a beat. "Is everything okay?"

"All weekend, if you're able. I could pick them up before the party so you don't have to take them there. Spencer's caught some stomach bug. He's been in the bathroom all day, and I don't want them to catch this if we can avoid it. I'm really hoping it's just some twelve-hour or twenty-four-hour thing."

Across the counter, Spencer grimaces, obviously not pleased with my choice of illness for him.

"Oh no. Well, sure. They can spend the weekend with Auntie Jo. I can take them to the party too, if he's still sick. My sister won't mind. Do you need me to pick them up from school today?" She clicks her tongue. "Oh. Shoot. I'm not sure I can make it in time, even if I leave right now, but I'll try."

"No. It's okay. Thanks, but don't worry about trying to rush over there. I'm sorry this is so last minute. I'll have Kaylee pick them up after school like normal. That way I can have her stop by to get their overnight bags and everything, and she can meet you at home. Does that work?"

"Yep, of course. Sounds like a plan. We'll rent movies or something. Her dropping them off gives me time to run to the store and get snacks."

"You don't have to get anything special."

"Aunt Jo code says I do," she teases. "Is there anything specific they'll want? Pizza for dinner okay?"

"They'll like whatever you get them. James has gotten pickier about things lately, but I really think that's just when he's home. His teachers say he eats lunch at school fine."

"Okay, I'll get a few options." I'm on speakerphone now. I can hear her typing something on her phone.

"You're the best. Seriously, thank you."

"You know I'm happy to watch them any time."

"When do you think you'll be home? After Kaylee picks them up, then stops by to get their things, she'll probably get to your house by three thirty or four. Is that enough time?"

"I should be able to make it by then. If she beats me there, just tell her the key is under the planter. Have her let herself in. The kids know where everything is. Can she stay with them for a while until I get there?"

"Yeah, totally. She usually stays until one of us gets home between five or six, so that won't be a problem. Listen, thank you so much. I owe you big time."

"You know my size." She laughs again. "And seriously, what are godmothers for? I'm happy to help. It's been a while since they had a sleepover at Aunt Jo's. Tell Spence I hope he gets to feeling better soon. Do you guys need anything else? I can order soup to be delivered."

"Thanks, but no. I'm still okay for the time being. I should go, though, so I can get their things together. I'll talk to you soon."

"Got it. I should probably get to the store, too. Traffic's a nightmare, and I don't want to be too late. Take care of yourself, okay? Love you guys."

"Love you, too." I end the call and place my phone down, tucking a piece of hair behind my ear. "That's taken care of."

Spencer stares at me. "You could've told her an illness that doesn't conjure images of me hugging a toilet bowl."

I shrug one shoulder. "Better than the truth. Now, come on. We need to get their things together before they get home."

AT JUST AFTER THREE O'CLOCK, I hear Kaylee's car pull into the driveway and rush to the door to meet them. She's still helping them unload their backpacks from the floorboard of her car when I approach.

"Hey, Mrs. E, I wondered why you weren't in class. Is everything okay?"

"Oh yeah. Spencer's a bit under the weather, so I had to leave early." I groan playfully. "It never ends." Looking down to face my children, I beam. It's painful to look into their eyes with guilt weighing on me so heavily. "Hey, guys. Have a good day at school?"

"Yes."

"Yeah, Mom."

The replies are instant, thoughtless, and unenthused. Oh, how I'd once envisioned the afternoons where they would be excited to tell me about their school days—when they'd rush home and give me a complete rundown of their activities, the friends they'd made, and all the fun they'd had.

Instead, this is what I've come to expect. Getting them to tell me anything about their days is like pulling teeth.

"Well, I have a surprise for you," I tell them, wrapping them each in a one-arm hug on the lawn.

"What is it?" Ava asks. "Did you get us a treat? Is it Starbucks?"

"Or a puppy?" James has been obsessed with puppies lately, so it's no shock to me that's exactly where his mind goes.

"No, not a puppy. Or Starbucks." I pat their heads, ruffling their hair. "Don't look so disappointed. It's something better."

Their faces brighten, waiting.

"How would you two like to spend the weekend with your Aunt Jo?"

"What? Really?" Ava cries, eyes wide. "Yes!"

James is slightly less enthused, but he smiles anyway. "What will we do?"

"Well, I have it on good authority that Aunt Jo has a very special weekend planned for you. And your dad and I will pick you up Sunday afternoon." I look up at Kaylee when she shuts the car door, brushing a bit of her caramel hair over her shoulder, arms folded across her chest. "Would you mind taking the kids to Jo's for me? Do you remember where it is?"

"Yeah, of course," she says. "Do you mean right now?"

"Yeah, if you don't mind. Spencer has come down with a stomach bug, and I don't want them to catch it."

"Oh." She takes half a step back from me as if I might be contaminated, too. "Yeah, of course. Um..." She looks down at James. "I think James had to pee before we got here, though. Should I...take him somewhere else? I'm not sure he'll make the full trip to Jo's."

I glance back at the house, then down at James. "No, of course not. Do you still need to go potty, James?"

"Mm-hmm." He nods, shuffling in place as if he just remembered.

"Okay, just a second. Let me just go warn your dad we're coming, okay? So he can get in the bedroom and shut the door. It'll be okay."

I hold up a hand, instructing them to wait there.

"They're coming inside," I tell Spencer when I find him waiting in the kitchen.

A vein in his neck bulges, his eyes traveling to the basement door. "*What?* Why? We made sure all their stuff was ready so they wouldn't."

"I know, but James needs to use the bathroom. I can't exactly tell him to hold it."

"That's *exactly* what you're going to have to do."

Heat creeps up my neck as I draw in a long breath. "Listen, we don't have time for this. James has to pee. There's no way around it. They're going to come inside. If she hears the kids up here moving around, I'm worried she might do something to draw attention to herself. That's the last thing we need right now. So, I need you to go down there and keep her quiet. We'll shut the bedroom door and tell them you're in there. He'll potty, and I'll get them out of here as quickly as I can."

He's quiet for a moment, his fingers tapping on the granite of the island.

"Come on, Spencer. We don't have much time."

"Right." He moves to the basement door, apprehension drawing lines across his forehead.

"It'll be okay," I promise, searching for the disinfectant spray under the sink to make our fake story more convincing. "Just keep her quiet, no matter what it takes."

I catch one last glimpse at his face as he shuts the door, then I move into the hall to pull our bedroom door closed. As I do, I hear the front door open, followed by the soft sounds of their voices.

"*Mom?*" James whines.

"Mrs. E?" Kaylee calls. "Sorry, he's really gotta go."

Before I can make it back down the hall, James's footsteps barrel toward me. He zips past and into the bathroom, shutting the door without a word. I emerge into the kitchen, then the living room where I find Kaylee and Ava waiting. Ava's backpack rests at her feet. My heart pounds in my ears, overriding my effort to listen for any sounds from our prisoner.

"Is Daddy going to be okay?" Ava asks, her wide eyes filled with so much innocence it breaks my heart.

"Oh yeah. He's going to be fine, sweetie. He's just not feeling well right now." I set the disinfectant spray on the end table next to the couch to avoid them noticing my hands trembling, then gesture toward the overnight bags near the door. "I packed your bags already."

"Did you remember Ellie?" she asks. Her pink elephant she's had since she was born.

"Of course I did. I made sure to put Ellie *and* Mr. Twinkles in there for you, just in case." I swipe a finger across my upper lip, drying the sweat gathered there. I need to keep talking to drown out any noise. "And you can just leave your backpacks at home. Do you have homework or anything?"

"No," she says. "Just a book to read."

I swallow. *Come on, James. Come on.* "Okay. Which book?"

"It's called *Wish*. I think it's about a dog."

"Great. Well, you can take that with you if you want to read it with Aunt Jo. Just be sure not to lose it. Or, if you want to leave it, we'll do it on Sunday night after you're back home." It feels like a lifetime away. What will my life look like on Sunday? For the first time in my life, I don't have an answer to that question.

Kaylee brushes a piece of hair out of Ava's eyes. "I can help her read it if you'd like."

James flushes the toilet down the hall. *Thank God.*

"That sounds nice. Doesn't it, Ava? If Jo isn't home when you get there, you guys could definitely do that. She may be there before you arrive, though, so if she is you can just—"

THUD. THUD. THUD.

A banging sound from the basement interrupts us.

My heart races in my chest, rattling against my ribs.

Kaylee's eyes widen. "What was that?"

"The pipes," I offer, my voice powerless. "Sounded like the pipes." I clear my throat. "Probably where James was washing his hands. They do that sometimes when we use hot water. I'm doing laundry, too."

"Hmm. I've never noticed," Kaylee says, glancing around the room. To my relief, she doesn't say anything else.

I clasp my hands together in front of me with a sharp inhale as James appears. "Okay, guys, why don't we get your bags. Can I have hugs and kisses?"

The kids give me a hug and kiss, and I grab both of their bags, leading them toward the door. I pull it open and usher them outside, squeezing my eyes shut when the door finally closes behind us.

"Mom, I'm hungry," James says.

"Me too," Ava chirps.

"Okay, well, Aunt Jo will have plenty of snacks for you when you get to her house. It won't take long to get there, alright?"

"But I want a snack now," he whines.

"Right, well, why don't you get buckled in and I'll go see if I can find something for you to eat on the way?"

"Yes!" James cheers, jerking his folded arm down with a victorious motion.

"I think I have a bag of veggie chips in my car," Kaylee offers, looking at me. "I don't mind if they snack on them if it's okay with you."

"That would be great, Kaylee." I pat her arm. "Thank you."

"Sure. No problem."

When we reach her car, she takes one side and I take the other as we help the kids get situated and buckled in. "If Jo isn't there when you arrive, there's a spare key under the planter. Just make yourself at home—the kids know where everything is. She should be there soon. Just call me if there are any issues."

"Okay. No worries."

"*I'm starving!*" James cries, rubbing his tummy.

Kaylee chuckles and grabs the bag of chips from her front seat, passing them back to the kids. "You have to share with each other, okay? I only have one bag."

"We will," he agrees, mouth already full, as Ava reaches for a chip.

"Okay, you guys." I stretch to kiss their heads. "Be good for Kaylee and Aunt Jo. I'll call you before bed. I love you." Stepping back, I lean down into the car so I can get a better look at them, blowing more kisses their way. "Miss you already."

They're blissfully unbothered, too busy shoveling handfuls of the colorful vegetable chips into their mouths.

"Thanks again, Kaylee. Be safe."

"You too," she calls, easing into the car and starting it up. She shuts the door and rolls down both windows on the driver's side. "See you Monday, Mrs. E. Wave to your mom, guys."

They do, waving wildly as the car backs out of the driveway.

This could be the last time I see them.

The thought hits me square in the gut, stealing my breath. If the police find out what we've done, if Heidi tells them what's happened, I could've just experienced my last moment with my babies.

The last time I'll kiss their heads and breathe in their sweet scents.

I wave harder, choking back tears. *Please remember me this way, sweet babies. Please remember how much I loved you.*

This won't be the last time, I promise myself. *It won't.*

I can't give up on them.

Now, more than ever before, I realize how badly we need this to all go away. There has to be a solution, even if I can't see it yet. Once they're gone, I return to the house. Resting my back against the door, I puff out a breath, wiping sweat from my brow and tears from my cheeks.

Somehow, we made it.

Somehow, that actually worked.

I lift their backpacks from where they dropped them on the floor and deliver them to their bedrooms. Back in the kitchen, I open the basement door slowly, listening.

How does he talk to her when I'm not around?

The light down below is eerie and ominous; its yellow glow, combined with dark shadows in every direction, is the stuff of nightmares. I finger the collar of my shirt, easing into the stairwell a bit farther.

"They're gone," I call cautiously. My breathing is so loud I can't hear myself think. "Spencer?"

Where is he? Did something happen?

I squeeze the doorknob, watching and listening for any signs of movement. With another step onto the landing, the musty smell hits me. It's familiar but worse now, somehow.

The basement is too quiet. Too dark.

I knock softly on the wall. "Spence?"

Thwomp.

Thwomp.

Thwomp.

Someone takes slow, careful steps toward the stairs. I grip the door, trying and failing to steady my breath.

"Spencer? Is that you?"

What a silly question. Of course it's him.

Who else would it be? She's tied up.

But...what if she's not? What if it's not Spencer?

What if she broke free? Attacked him?

Killed him?

I vacillate between descending the stairs to see what's going on and shutting the door to run for my life, without much time to decide.

This image, this waiting, the sounds of someone drawing nearer...it's too much.

Finally, I force a breath of air from my lungs as Spencer appears. He's slow to climb the stairs, and when I get a better look at him, I spy the blood near his temple.

I step backward into the kitchen. "What happened? What was that noise?"

"She headbutted me"—he touches his fingers to the wound gently, wincing—"while trying to bang her head on the post to make noise."

When he follows me into the kitchen and pulls the door shut, he's wearing a grim expression. I study the bloody gash, which doesn't seem serious but is bleeding quite a lot.

"Let me see. Are you okay?" I ask as he leans down.

When he answers, his tone is dry. "Never better."

CHAPTER EIGHT

SPENCER

Andi is staring at me as if I've grown another head. Meanwhile, my one and only head throbs as hot sticky blood trickles down my temple.

"It's fine. I'm all right." I move around to the sink and pull a paper towel from the roll, wetting it slightly and pressing it to the wound just above my eyebrow. "What did you tell them?"

"That you were sick, just like we planned."

"I meant about the noise." I turn back to her, the cool cloth stinging my raw skin. "I'm assuming they heard it? Exactly like I was worried they would."

"Oh, yeah, they heard the banging. It was muffled from up here. I told them it was the pipes. I think they believed me. Why wouldn't they?"

"For both our sakes, I hope they did. Now, we need to decide how we're going to do this. She's becoming more hostile by the minute. I was thinking...if we kill her, we can't bury her in the backyard. It will be the first place the police look if they think we're involved. But we also can't be seen carrying her out. So, we need to clear out the garage some, we'll back into it, and we can take some of our old stuff to the landfill. That way, it seems like that's all we were doing. Getting rid of some old junk. Then we can take her body to the lake."

I see the way she's staring at me, her horror becoming more pronounced with every sentence I say, but there's no more time for messing around. I don't have the time or patience to hold her hand through this anymore. Heidi made it very clear once our children are home, she'll never stop. We have to get rid of her once and for all.

"The...the landfill will be closed," she says softly.

Shit. She's right. "Okay. Well, we'll say we didn't realize it closed so early. It'll be fine."

"But... We've already told people you were sick. Why would you be going to the landfill?"

"No one has to know I was with you."

"Oh, so now this is all on me?" She's nearing hysterics, her eyes bloodshot and filled with tears. She chews the inside of her lip nervously.

"Okay, forget the landfill idea. We'll say you were going to get me medicine. I rode with you."

"Why would we have to back the car into the garage, then?"

"*Because...*" I try to think, chomping down on my lower lip. "Because I was sick and you were bored, so you cleaned out the garage."

She looks down, obviously disappointed.

"Come on, aren't you always telling me we should organize it so we can park one of the cars inside of it? We could say you finally decided to do it yourself? And besides, this is all hypothetical and only happens *if* the police come around asking questions. For all we know, they won't."

Andi steels herself, her shoulders straightening, horror-stricken expression washing away. "Fine. Okay. How do you know we won't get caught trying to dump her body?"

"I don't, I guess. But I think it's our best bet. We'll park down by the water, wait until no one's around, and then drop her in."

She blinks rapidly like she might pass out. "Will she... Will she float? Should we use rocks or bricks or something to...to help?"

"I have a few cinder blocks and a tarp in the garage. We'll wrap her up with those."

She swallows, folding her arms across her chest. She can't bear to look at me. I can't say I blame her.

For the record, I fully realize we're talking about another person. A human person who has done nothing wrong other than threaten my happiness, my family, my freedom. I never thought it would end this way when the affair started. Of course I didn't. If I had, I would've walked away the night we met.

Andi still looks as if she's going to be sick, but she doesn't argue. I think she's lost some of her fight because of all this. Some of the fiery spirit I've always loved about her.

She's kind to a fault, but challenge her at something she's passionate about? Or worse, do something to hurt someone she loves? She can be absolutely fervent. And whip-smart. A terrifying combination that's certain to bring you to shame.

Will that side of her ever come back? I truly don't know.

My phone buzzes in my pocket, interrupting my thoughts, and I pull it out and stare at the screen.

Linda Smith.

"It's my boss."

"Answer it," Andi whispers.

My fingers are icy as I swipe one across my screen and press the phone to my ear. "Linda, hi."

"Hi. Where are you, Spencer?"

"I'm...at home. I had to take the afternoon off."

"Oh, that's right." I can hear the sounds of her quick typing through the phone. She's lightning fast and only half listening, as usual. "I forgot you told me that. No problem. I'm just calling to see if you forwarded the hotel confirmation for our Dallas trip yet? I need to get it submitted to corporate, but I can't find it."

Shit.

She can't find it because I never sent it.

I never sent it because I never made it.

"I'm sorry, Linda. I don't remember if I sent it or not. I'll double-check and get it forwarded to you right now."

"That'd be great. Did you get east-facing rooms? You know I like to watch the sun rise."

"I...I'm not sure if they had any left, but I think I requested it. Sorry. Let me just get to my computer." I run a finger over my bottom lip, making no move to get my laptop when a thought occurs to me. The trip is next week. We leave on Monday. "Actually, while I have you on the phone, I'm not sure I'm going to be able to make the trip."

The typing stops. She's quiet for a beat. "Why not?"

"I'm sick. I'm not sure I'll be better by Monday."

Quickly, she returns to typing. "Oh. Well, how sick?

Have you gone to the doctor? I'm sure they can fix you right up. I really need you there."

"I know. I'm sorry, I just—"

In front of me, Andi is waving her hands wildly, shaking her head. *No,* she mouths.

"Actually, can I call you back?"

She stops typing again, making no attempt to hide her groan. Her tone is clipped. "No need. Just forward the reservations. We'll touch base on Sunday about the trip. Rest up."

With that, she ends the call and I place my phone on the island. "What the hell was that?"

Andi pins me with an accusing look. "You can't cancel your trip."

"Well, I can't exactly go."

"Yes. You can. You have to. We need to have this all handled by Sunday evening when the kids come home, and after that, we have to go forward like everything is normal. That's the only way we're going to get out of this. *If* we do."

"Fine. I agree. She said we'll check back in on Sunday. I'll tell her then that I'm better and will be able to go. For now, I need to book our hotel rooms so she doesn't get suspicious."

I cross the room and pick up my laptop bag from the banquette bench by the bay window. I pull the silver MacBook out, placing it on the island to search for a suitable reservation for the two of us.

When I, thankfully, find a room Linda will approve of, I book it on the corporate card, then locate another less-impressive one for me in the same building. I forward the confirmations to Linda and cross my fingers she doesn't check the confirmation date and realize I lied.

Then again, I have bigger problems.

When I look up, Andi is filling the teakettle. It's what she always does when she's nervous or upset. I often joke that she must've been a little old British woman in a past life.

Now, I can't find it in me to joke about anything.

"We could give her sleeping pills," I offer. She shuts off the water and turns to face me. "It would be easy. Painless." My eyes flick to the kettle. "We could crush them up in her tea. I could suffocate her once she's asleep. No blood that way."

She winces but carries on working, refusing to meet my gaze. "She won't drink it," she says, placing the small metal lid on the kettle and walking toward the stove. "I tried to bring her something to drink earlier, and she spat it in my face. She doesn't trust us. Can't say I blame her."

"When did you try to bring her a drink?"

"When you were gone."

I bristle at her words. "You didn't tell me that. You said you brought her a blanket, not a drink. *She spat it in your face?* You should've told me, Andi."

"Don't bother lecturing me on the importance of truthfulness, Spencer. Clearly, you have no room to talk."

Fair enough. I take half a step back, giving her space at the stove. "I still think it's worth a try. She might trust me. I may be able to get her to drink it."

She shrugs one shoulder, turning the knob on the stove.

Click.

Click.

Click.

The gas flame ignites.

"I can't see why she'd trust you after all you've done, but

by all means, have at it." Her eyes widen, then narrow, and she turns her head to look at me. She spins around, resting her back against the edge of the countertop. "She will take pills, though."

"What are you talking about?"

"I gave her pills. Just some ibuprofen. To help with her pain and the swelling."

"You *what?*" I shout, louder than I intend to. I hate raising my voice. "What else did you do? What else don't I know?"

"Should I ask you the same thing?" She grips her hip. "I thought it would get her to trust us. That we could find some way to make peace with all of this. So it didn't come to"—she gestures around the room, the chaos of our lives—"this. More than that, it was the right thing to do. She must be in terrible pain, Spencer. It's the least I could do for her."

"Yeah, maybe. But you should've talked to me first. She could've hurt you."

"I'm fine. And now we know"—she lowers her voice slightly—"*she'll take pills.* Maybe we could just *give* her the sleeping pills instead of trying to slip them in her tea. It's been a while. The pills I gave her will be wearing off soon enough. We could just tell her it's for the pain." Her eyes dart between mine, full of hope.

"Yeah, I mean, it's not a bad idea. The problem is we'll have to give her quite a few to make sure she sleeps through it. I only have my over-the-counter sleep aids. If we could crush several pills up in her drink, that's one thing, but I hardly think we'll be able to offer her a handful of pills without her getting suspicious." I twist my mouth in thought. "Maybe something stronger would be better."

"Any ideas?"

I have one, but she's not going to like it. "There's nothing we can get over the counter that will be strong enough for what we need. And it's going to be impossible to get a prescription at this time on a Friday. Not to mention how suspicious that would look and the paper trail it would leave. But...there might be another way."

"What are you talking about?"

"I... Look, it's not the best option, but it might be our only one."

"Tell me."

"I could get a number from Tyler at work. Someone who'd have what we need and could be discreet."

Her head jerks backward. "You can't be serious. *A drug dealer?*"

The horror of what I'm suggesting is evident in her expression. It's not like I'm excited about it. Despite the stereotypes about my industry, I've never done drugs in my life. Not even pot. I drink sparingly to get me through social events, but my parents are both functioning alcoholics and I have no desire to follow in their footsteps. Drugs have always been a line I'm unwilling to cross. It's one of the many things Andi and I agree on.

That being said, I know many of the guys I work with do choose to partake. No judgment to them; I don't think I'm any better than them—*well, maybe better than Tyler*—I just know it's not the lifestyle I want for me and my family.

"It could work. I'm just saying it's an option. One of our only options."

She stares at the wound on my head and I lower the

paper towel, the white paper now dyed a light shade of crimson.

"What?" I put my hand up to where she's staring.

"Just wondering how hard you bumped your head," she says plainly, then turns to walk away, rounding the island. "I can't believe you're even considering this."

"Is that really the most surprising revelation of the day?" I point out.

She purses her lips. "Maybe not. But... Well, I'm not having a drug dealer come to our house."

"Of course not. I'll go meet them somewhere. Downtown, maybe."

"Fine," she says with a wave of her wrist. "Whatever. Let's just get this taken care of."

"Great. I'll text Tyler." I wait for her to tell me not to, but when she doesn't, I pull out my phone and search my contacts for his name. When I land on it, I type out the text.

Hey. Can I get a number for your guy?

I add a leaf emoji, then a puff-of-smoke emoji and press send.

Within minutes, I receive a response. Well, sort of a response. A phone number. No name. A sort of *hang-loose* emoji. Nothing else.

I flip it around to show Andi. She nods, looking away bitterly. She's not happy with me, but she hasn't left yet. I have to find the positives, however they come.

I copy the number, close out of the message, and start a new one.

My cheeks burn as I realize I have no idea what to say to a dealer. I only know what I've seen in movies.

> Hi. Got this number from a friend. I need to buy something.

I press send.

Weed still isn't legal in Tennessee, but it's a far cry from murder, so if the police search my phone and find this text, I'm willing to take my chances. I'll tell them Andi and I had a night alone. I wasn't feeling well and wanted something to help with my nausea. It helps with that...doesn't it?

They don't have to know that's not actually what I'm buying.

My adrenaline spikes as I close out of the message, my fingers trembling. I swipe through my phone nervously, waiting for a response.

When I spot my social media app, curiosity gets the best of me. I open it and type her name.

"I'm going to check how the post is doing."

"What post?" Andi comes to stand next to me, peering over my shoulder.

"Her social media..." I land on the post and scroll down. There are over one thousand comments, mostly from followers wishing her good luck and commending her for prioritizing her mental health. "Looks like we might've actually pulled that off."

Andi looks less than pleased but reaches for my phone, reading through the comments quietly.

When the screen changes and a call from an unknown number appears, she hands it back to me with wide, terrified eyes. "Who's calling you?"

"No idea. It could be Linda again."

It's not. We both know it. I put the phone to my ear. "Hello?"

"Who's this?"

The man's tone is soft. Unusually calm.

"Um, who is this?"

"You texted me. Who gave you this phone number?"

My stomach flips. *The dealer,* I mouth to Andi, who cups a hand over her lips and spins away with a yelp.

"Um, sorry, it's... I got it from a friend. Tyler. He said you could hook me up with some pills."

I'm surprised at the effortless way it comes out of my mouth.

He pauses. "Sure. Where are you?"

"Nashville. Donelson area. I could meet you downtown."

"What are you looking for?"

"Something to knock me out for a few hours. I can't sleep, and when I do sleep, I get these migraines—"

He chuckles, interrupting me. "Look man, I'm not a doctor. I don't care why you need it. Meet me in an hour. I'll send you the address."

"Okay, awesome. Thank you."

"And, hey."

"Yeah?"

His voice darkens. "If you bring anyone with you, I'll kill you both on the spot."

"Right. I...I won't be doing that, I can promise you."

"Better not."

The call cuts off before I can respond.

Within seconds, an address appears on my screen.

"Here we go." I spin it around to Andi, who simply nods.

"Change your clothes into something else. You don't want to dress too nicely. He'll think we have a lot of money."

Joke would be on him, I think, but I don't argue as I turn around and hurry to the bedroom to change.

I try not to let her notice my hands shaking. I'm already planning to murder someone today. What's one more crime?

As I'm pulling on a pair of sweatpants, I hear my phone buzzing from the kitchen. The dull hum is impossible to miss in the otherwise silent house.

We jog back into the kitchen and she picks it up, handing it to me with a worried glare. This time, a number is displayed. Is it the dealer again? I can't remember if this was the phone number Tyler gave me.

"Hello?"

"Is this Spencer?"

I swallow. Definitely not the dealer. I recognize the voice...but from where?

"Uh, yeah. Who's this?"

"Hey, man, sorry to bother you. Linda said you're out sick. This is Dave Gibbons."

An agent from work. I release a breath. Linda must've asked him to call or something. I wave a hand at Andi, letting her know everything's okay.

Work, I mouth.

"Oh, hey, Dave. What's up?" It's pretty unusual to hear from other agents in general as an assistant. Mostly, I hear from Linda; her boss, Stewart; or the other assistants.

I rack my brain, trying to decide why he'd be calling.

I don't have to wonder for long.

"Listen, weird question... Do you know Heidi Dawson?"

CHAPTER NINE

ANDI

The blood drains from Spencer's face, his breathing stopping as he lowers the phone from his ear and puts it on speaker.

"Um. Of course I know Heidi Dawson."

No. I shake my head. Why would he say that? Why would he admit to knowing her?

"I mean, I know *of* her, at least," he adds quickly, backtracking a bit. "I wouldn't say I *know her*, know her. But I know her work and that she's a client." He pinches the bridge of his nose with his fingers.

What is he doing? This is worse than just admitting to knowing her. This is so much worse. If whoever is on the other line doesn't already know about the affair, they're sure to suspect it now.

"Okay," the man says slowly.

"Why do you ask?"

"Well, it's the strangest thing. She's apparently left the country to go on some sort of, like, *Eat, Pray, Love* situation.

She emailed Sarah and her manager, Evelyn Stroud—not sure if you know her—and said she needed to take some time off."

"Oh, wow. Well, that doesn't sound good. I hope she's okay," Spencer says. He sounds terrified. I hope Dave doesn't register it.

"Yeah, me too. Sarah's out of the office because her daughter's giving birth, so she has my contact info in her out-of-office message. I just got a call from Evelyn asking about you."

"About me? Why?"

"Well." He chuckles as if he doesn't believe what he's saying. "Apparently Heidi told her she was going to see you this afternoon."

Spencer's eyes fall to me, languishing in hopelessness. He's ready to give up. I see it, and it makes me want to fight more.

I wave my hand in a fanning motion, as if I'm trying to waft the scent of a five-star dish toward me. *Wrap it up. You don't know anything,* I mouth.

He swipes a hand over his forehead. "Me? Why would she be coming to see me? Is she sure she meant me? It's a common name."

"Yeah, Heidi told her she was flying into town to meet with Spencer Edwards. The manager seemed certain you worked for our agency. I told her it didn't make sense, that you were just an assistant"—Spencer's shoulders tense—"and not even Sarah's assistant. It wouldn't make sense."

"I... Yeah. Well, I'm not sure what to say. I never spoke with her about any meeting. Like you said, I'd have no reason to. I left work sick around noon today, so if she was coming to see me for whatever reason, she probably missed me. Evelyn should try to call her."

"Yeah, she did. Her phone's turned off." He grunts. "Alright. Well. Strange. I'll let her know anyway. It's probably nothing. Another actress on a bender, if you ask me. Is it okay to give Evelyn your number in case she wants to touch base? Hear it from you?"

"S-sure."

"Cool. Thanks, man. Feel better."

"You too." He doesn't realize he's just told Dave to *feel better too,* as the remainder of the blood seems to drain from his face. We watch the screen go dark, the call over, and my heart sinks.

He curses, dropping the phone and slamming both hands down onto the countertop.

"What do we do?" I ask.

"I don't know." He stares down at the counter, gripping it as if he may fall over.

"What else do you think she told her manager?"

"I don't know."

"About the affair?"

"*I don't know.*" He checks his watch and curses again. "I can't deal with this right now. I need to leave if I'm still going to make it in time."

He moves around me, grabbing the keys from the island and hurrying toward the door. Before he exits, he turns back. "Stay up here, okay? Please. Leave her alone."

"I will," I promise.

"Swear it?"

"I swear," I lie.

CHAPTER TEN

SPENCER

It only occurs to me after I've parked in the parking garage that I have no idea who I'm looking for or where exactly we're supposed to be meeting. Inside? Outside? Is it his apartment? An office building?

I can't exactly ask someone if they've seen him.

Excuse me, have you seen anyone who looks like a drug dealer around here? No, no reason at all. Just a question. Actually, it's sort of a scavenger hunt situation. All we still need is a photo with a drug dealer. Think you can help me out?

I roll my eyes and pull out my phone, considering texting Tyler to ask what he looks like, but decide against it.

I'm two minutes late as I round the corner of the building where he asked to meet. It's an Italian restaurant. The scent of hearty tomato sauce and garlic hits my nose as someone exits the front door. I look around, searching for the guy.

Not an easy task.

The sidewalk is bustling with people. Tourists, mostly. Half a dozen bachelorette parties, complete with matching sashes and cowgirl hats, most completely shit-faced while it's just now five o'clock. Businessmen and women talking on their cell phones, moving fast, not making eye contact. On the street, I see three pedal taverns—more bachelorette parties screaming obscenities to the crowded sidewalk.

A musician plays his guitar on the corner, the speakers on either side of him filling the street with his voice—he's pretty good, at least. Around him, people stand and gawk, clapping when he finishes and tossing dollar bills into a tin bucket on the ground.

I spin around, nearly bumping into a homeless man and his dog as they move past me.

"Sorry."

I glance back in the direction from which I came. Have I been stood up? Am I too late? The musician starts singing again, the music making it hard to think.

"Hey, man."

I hear the voice coming from behind me and spin around.

"Hey."

Whoever I'd been expecting, this is not him. The man is dressed in a fitted business suit, his thick, brown hair slicked back. The dark facial hair on his cheeks and chin is neatly trimmed with crisp lines. He looks like he should be selling stocks on Wall Street or cologne in a TV commercial, not pills on a street corner.

He moves forward with a confidence that makes me uneasy. "Long time no see."

I furrow my brows. "Sorry? You may have the wrong person."

"Nah, I don't." He snaps his fingers, pointing at me. "You're Tyler's friend, right?"

My shoulders drop. "Yes. That's right. You're..." The question hangs in the air.

"Yep." He watches as an older couple moves past and waves at them. It's as if he doesn't have a care in the world. "How's the family?"

"Um, great. Yours?"

"Perfect." He smirks, then jerks his head to the side, leading me closer to the building. When I draw closer—but not too close—he lowers his voice and shoves both hands into the pockets of his slacks. "Six hundred bucks."

"Six hundred?" I had no idea what drugs cost, and I was only prepared to pay around a hundred. The look on his face tells me he isn't planning to bargain.

"I... I don't have that much on me."

He runs a tongue over his bottom lip. "Well, that's—" A couple exits the Italian restaurant, and he pauses to smile at them. "That's gonna be a real problem. I know you didn't waste my time coming out here. Tyler said you were good for it."

"No, of course. I am. I just need to go to the ATM."

"Lead the way, boss." He drags his hands from his pockets and gestures forward. I swallow, absolutely certain I'm going to be mugged. Why hadn't I thought to ask how much I would need?

We find an ATM just a few stores down, and I sneak between a group of visibly drunk men wearing cowboy boots to get to it. The man hangs back, leaning against the brick wall and scrolling mindlessly through his iPhone.

With the cash folded in my hand, like I've seen in the movies, I walk back out to the street to meet him.

He studies me with amusement, pushing his phone back into his pocket. "Everything okay?"

"Yeah. Yep. I'm not a cop." I have no idea why I say that.

"Well, now it kind of seems like you are a cop," he says, chuckling under his breath. "Breathe, man. We're fine." He checks over his shoulder. "Tyler vouched for you, I told you."

"Right. Sorry."

"You've never done this before."

I'm not sure if he's asking or telling me. "No."

"I didn't think so."

He holds out his hand, rubbing his fingers together.

"The...pills?" I ask, keeping my voice low.

"Cash first." It's the first time his smile disappears. Down to business.

"Right." I hand him the folded bills, and he turns them over in his hands, counting them slowly. When he's satisfied, he shoves the cash into the inside pocket of his blazer and retrieves a small bag of pills.

He places them into my palm without a hint of worry. "Nice to see you again."

I shove the pills into my pocket and step back, checking over my shoulder. "Yeah. See you around."

"I'm sure I will." He chuckles, then waves at the two lanes of traffic stopped at a red light as he crosses the road, buttoning his blazer. I don't dare look at the pills as I make my way back toward the parking garage, weaving in and out of people. As the Friday night crowd descends on downtown

Nashville, it becomes nearly unrecognizable. I want to be as far away from this place by then as possible.

The irony of the statement has me laughing to myself as I climb into my car. *Wouldn't want to find myself in any danger...*

As I start the car, I can't help celebrating.

I made it.

I did it.

We might actually get away with this.

I drive the whole way across town with the music blaring, occasionally patting my pocket to make sure the pills are still there.

They are.

This is all going to work out.

CHAPTER ELEVEN

ANDI

Downstairs once again, I find Heidi resting with her head against the post. Her eyes crack open when I near the bottom. It smells different down here, and I realize she's used the bathroom on herself. Her jeans and the comforter are now soaked with wet spots. I cover my mouth and nose, the scent burning my eyes.

She grins as if she's enjoying seeing me miserable.

After all I've done for her...

I move closer, grabbing the pool stick on my way, and rip the tape off of her mouth. This time, I make no effort to be gentle. "If you scream, I'll use this. I swear I will." When she doesn't, I go on, "You should've told us you needed to use the restroom. Spencer was just down here."

"Why? What were you going to do? Bring me a bucket? Undress me and help me sit down on it?" She shakes her head. "No. I want you to clean this up. This reminder that I'm a person. I hope you can never get the scent completely out. I hope this place reeks of me for the rest of your life, Andi. I hope you smell me in every corner of this house."

I pull the shirt down away from my face, refusing to give her the satisfaction of my disgust. "It didn't have to be like this. I was trying to help you. I was trying to find another way."

"There was never going to be another way." She stares at me with a sort of deranged disbelief. *"Tell me you get that.* From the second he locked me down here, I knew what was going to happen. I wasn't going to beg for my life or make promises when I knew it would never matter. From the second I fell down those stairs, I was a dead woman."

I see the pain of the words in her eyes then, though she's trying to hide it. Nearly succeeding, too. I see now why she's an actress.

"I don't believe that, and I don't think you do either. There had to be some part of you that believed you could convince him to let you go."

"What part of any of this looks like we'd be able to have a rational conversation?" She grimaces. "Yeah, you know what? Actually, I may have believed I had a shot when he brought you down here. When I met you, I thought, *There's no way she will let him get away with this. She's a woman. A mother.* You gave me a bit of hope, but I realized pretty quickly it was useless."

"I tried to help you!" I cry, smacking a hand into my chest.

Her smile is bitter. "I'm sure you need to believe that you did all you could, but the truth is, you could've let me out. You could save me right now if you wanted to, Andi. You've had the opportunity twice now. So, whatever happens to me, it's on you as much as it is him."

"You're right. But it's not that simple. Whatever decision I make affects my kids. He's their father."

"*And you're their mother,*" she snaps. "You're *a* mother. A woman. How can you be okay with any of this? What if it was your daughter? What if some monster had your daughter chained down here?"

The thought makes me dizzy. I squeeze my eyes shut, forcing away the haunting images.

"Stop it."

"You'd want someone to save her, wouldn't you? If there was a woman there, a woman who could help her, you'd count on her to save your baby, wouldn't you?" She pauses, watching me—begging for the first time. "*Wouldn't you?*"

I need her to stop. To stop talking. To stop saying what she's saying.

This isn't as simple as she's making it seem.

"Andi, you cannot let him get away with this."

I close my eyes, trying to drown out her words. I need to think. It's Spencer. I can't hurt him. I can't let her go if I know it'll ruin his life. More than that, she's sure to tell the police I was here, too. That I didn't let her go right away. Maybe not the first time—but now? There's no way she won't blame me, too.

If we both go to prison, what would happen to the kids? That can't be the last time I see them. I won't survive it.

What would happen to Jo, who'd end up raising them? What will it do to the career and business she's worked so hard to build?

Even if, by some miracle, we were to get off without

prison time, the repercussions are vast. The community would hate us. They'd make the kids' lives miserable. I'd lose my job, no doubt. Parents don't want women who are capable of things like this teaching their kids. Spencer would lose his job, too. We'd lose the house. Lose the cars.

By letting her go, I'd essentially be setting fire to our lives. There is no going back from here. This moment is the fault line. The point of no return.

"You've given us no choice. I *am* protecting my babies by refusing to let you go. Because you've made it clear you intend to burn our lives to the ground if we let you out of here."

She sneers. "I should've known. I had you pegged right from the start. The apologist. *Stand by your man...* to hell with everyone else." She leans forward, then launches back, smacking her head against the post behind her.

THUD.

THUD.

"Stop it!"

"No. If you won't let me go, I will make sure my DNA is on every surface in this basement. My blood." She smacks her head against it again, so blood splatters against the totes behind her. She hardly even winces, so full of adrenaline. "My hair. My piss. My shit. Every surface is going to have a piece of me. Even once I'm gone, even as you try to convince yourself you did what you had to do, all so you can sleep at night, you'll always know I'm still here. And when the police come, because they will, they'll find me. And they'll find out what you did. What he did. They'll make sure he never hurts anyone else. No matter how much bleach you have, no matter how much you scrub, you'll never find it all."

I wince as she takes her leg, damp with urine, and drags it across the floor slowly. The stench of excrement hits my nose. She's going to cost me my family.

I'm only trying to help, and this is how she thanks me?

I hate her. I hate her. I hate her.

"Oh, real mature," I spit, choking. "You know what, Heidi?"

She stops squirming and looks up at me. I throw the pool stick down away from her, then turn and stomp up the stairs, my body radiating with anger. I feel like a thumb in those old cartoons that's just been smashed—pulsing red like a heartbeat, *boom-boom, boom-boom.* When I reach the top step, I flip off the light again, plunging her into darkness.

Just before I shut the door, I shout down, "If it were my daughter, I'd tell her not to sleep with other people's husbands."

CHAPTER TWELVE

SPENCER

I walk into the house, triumphant, kicking my shoes off next to the door before I strut into the kitchen. "I did it," I call to my wife, whose back is to me as she scrubs her hands in the sink.

She turns around, her eyes bloodshot.

She's been crying.

"What's wrong?" I move forward, but she shakes her head and waves me away.

"Nothing. I just want to get this over with. You got the pills?"

"Yes. I did."

"Okay. Good. What are you planning to do?" She sounds almost robotic. Broken. I hate myself for what I've done to her.

"I'll have you give her the pills, like last time, and then when she's asleep, we'll suffocate her. It'll be the easiest way. She won't feel any pain. She'll only know she fell asleep."

She wraps her arms around herself, brushing her chin against her shoulder. "And then what?"

"Then we'll wrap her in the tarp with the cinder blocks and take the body to the lake."

"And you really don't think there's another way?"

I puff out a breath, giving my head a slow shake. "No. I'm sorry. There's no other way. We've both done too much at this point. If she gets the chance, she'll turn us both in, no question. We'll go to prison. We have to get rid of her."

She sighs, leaning forward onto the island, a wary look in her eyes. "Okay, well, let's see 'em."

I slip a hand into my pocket and pull out the bag, examining the pills for the first time. There are three in total—all small, round, and white. I run my thumb over each one.

She rests her hands on the granite top, clasping them together. "Did he ask any questions?"

"No. He told me Tyler said I was cool, so he wasn't worried."

"Did he tell you what they'll do?"

"No. I told him I needed something to knock me out so I could sleep. He said this'll do it."

"How much did you pay?"

"Six hundred dollars." I can't bear to meet her eyes as I say the words. That money would have nearly paid the entire year of Ava's dance tuition. It's a month's worth of car payments. It's money we didn't have to waste on three tiny pills, but what choice did I have?

"*What?*" She gives the exact reaction I expected.

"*I know.* I didn't expect it to be so much, but once I was there, how could I say no? We'd already come so far."

She kneads her forehead with her fingers. "Which account did you take it out of?"

"The main one. It'll be okay, I promise. Once we get rid of her, it'll be okay. We'll figure out the rest."

"All right." She waves a hand at me again. "Well, go take care of it. You can forget about me helping you. I'm not going down there again. She's shit all over herself, and I'm not dealing with it."

What the hell is she talking about? "Wait. You went down there again?"

"Yeah, I did. Don't lecture me right now. Just go."

I open the bag and pour the pills out into my hand, then head for the basement. It's pitch black for a few seconds as I feel along the wall for the light switch. As I step onto the landing at the top of the stairs, the rancid odor assaults my nostrils. I cough, my eyes stinging, as I cover my nose with my arm.

It's awful. Terrible.

It smells like something died.

The thought sobers me.

I breathe through my mouth as I walk down the steps. The smell is almost enough to make me vomit.

Almost.

"Well, well, well... The gang's all here." Her voice startles me, and I look up to find her smiling wickedly.

It takes me a second to realize *her mouth isn't taped.* Panic seizes me, propelling me forward as I dart across the room and toward where the roll of tape is lying on top of a tote.

"How did you get it off?" I demand, wagging the tape in her face.

"*I* didn't. Your pretty little wife took it off for me." She bats her eyelashes. "She *is* pretty, especially when she's angry."

"Don't talk about her," I grunt.

"It's men like you who are the problem, Spencer. Men who have a perfectly good life. A beautiful home, sweet kids, loving wife, and you still throw it away. What is it? Did you need to feel *like a man?*" She says the last three words in a seductive growl. My upper lip curls in disgust. "Was it worth it? Was any of this worth it?"

"*Of course not,*" I shout, angry at myself for giving in to her. It's exactly what she wants. "Is that what you want to hear? Of course it wasn't worth it. It could never be worth this. Now, shut up and take these pills before I change my mind about helping you." I eye the wooden post behind her, fresh blood soaking into the wood where she's obviously been banging her head into it again. She's absolutely batshit.

"*Medicine?* What for, doc?"

"For the pain. Andi said she gave you some earlier, but it's probably worn off by now. She wanted me to bring you something else."

She eyes them. "She brought me ibuprofen. They were red."

I run my finger over the pills. "This is something else, then. I don't know. She just said to bring them to you. Do you want them or not? I don't have all day."

She shakes her head. "No. I don't want them."

"What?"

"You heard me. I'm all set." She's so smug it kills me.

I cock my head to the side, lowering my voice. "What are

you talking about? There's no need to suffer. Take the pills, Heidi."

"Go fuck yourself." She spits at me; a thick glob of saliva lands on my shirt. I swipe it away angrily, cursing.

"Don't be so difficult. Just take the damn pills." I take hold of her face, trying to pry her jaw open by pressing on both sides of her cheeks. She turns her head sharply, chomping down on my thumb without warning. I yelp and jump back, nearly tossing the pills, but I somehow manage to stop myself.

Six hundred dollars.

"I said no, asshole."

I shake my head, anger radiating within me. My chest throbs, ready to explode. "Why do you have to be so stubborn? I'm trying to help you." I rub my thumb against my shirt, eyeing the teeth marks she left.

"Just making sure you never forget me." She winks.

I tear off a piece of tape and slap it over her mouth, refusing to meet her eyes again. Sometimes, I could swear she likes this.

CHAPTER THIRTEEN

ANDI

When Spencer disappears downstairs, I pull my phone out and end the recording I was trying to make. It had been a stupid idea anyway, trying to catch him on tape admitting to the crime. It was my safety net, one I hoped never to have to use, but that would provide me some peace of mind. Turns out, it didn't matter anyway. I couldn't get him to say anything that didn't also incriminate me.

I'll have you give her the pills, like last time...

We've both done too much. She'll turn us both in, no question...

It was as if he knew. Then again, my husband has always been the type to stumble into good luck. Until now, that is.

There's a struggle happening downstairs. I can't make out what they're saying, but I hear raised voices. Shouting. I've heard my husband shout more today than I have in the entire rest of the time I've known him, I think. I should go down and make sure he's okay, but I can't.

I can't stand to face her right now.

Just the thought of it has my blood boiling. So, I find a seat by the window and stare out, imagining how easily this could all go away. Everything good about my life could be stolen from me because of the man I love. The man I trusted.

I thought we'd built a good life. I take in the sight of the backyard, the treehouse where we have family campouts, the firepit where we roast marshmallows. A few years ago, Spencer surprised us with a projector, and we started having movie nights against the backdrop of the house.

There's a bubble-blowing lawn mower that James still loves to play with, though he's probably a bit too old, and the little playhouse with the working doorbell Ava adores.

Yesterday, I'd taken so much of this for granted: the easy afternoons spent with just the four of us playing board games, watching movies, and cooking dinner together.

The kids always love to help... Do I let them enough? Have I filled them with enough memories to last them forever if we're taken away from them?

Will they know how much I love them? *Obsessively. Dangerously.*

Will they understand how badly I wanted to protect them? How hard I have tried?

After a few minutes, I hear Spencer coming back up the stairs. He pulls the door open and steps into the kitchen, tossing the pills at the island with too much force. They scatter, and I stare at them as they slide and drop to the floor.

One.

Two.

Three.

The third one skids over near my foot.

"She didn't take them?" I bend forward to pick it up.

"No, she wouldn't. Didn't trust me, I guess. I said it was your idea, but she didn't believe me." He's speaking through tight lips, patches of crimson covering his neck and cheeks.

"Well, she may have believed you. I don't know that she trusts me anymore either. We didn't exactly end things on good terms when I was down there."

He grimaces as I turn the pill over in my hand.

"So, now what? What are we going to—" I cut myself off, lifting the pill closer to my face for a better look. I turn it between two fingers, reading the seven small letters running in a circle.

I gasp, then stand and hurry to find the others. Carefully, I pick up each pill and examine the letters running in a circle around its top. They're all the same.

"What's wrong?" Spencer moves closer, trying to make out what I'm looking at.

I shake my head in disbelief, locking my jaw. "They're aspirin, Spencer."

He reaches for one. "What? No."

"They're aspirin!" I shout, shoving all three pills into his palm. "He sold you three aspirin for six hundred dollars."

Spencer stares at the pills, turning one over in his hand to read what I just have. After a moment, his mouth goes slack. "I'm going to kill Tyler." The words fall flat in the silent room, and he looks up at me. "I'm so sorry."

I groan, cradling my head in my hands. "He must've known you had no idea what you were doing. What you were looking for." I can't stop the tears that prick my eyes.

"Please don't cry," he whispers, looking as helpless as I feel.

"Why did you do it, Spence?"

"What? The pills? You know why."

"No. *Her.* Why did you sleep with her? Why did you have the affair? Are you just that unhappy?" The tears are falling freely now, and I don't bother wiping them away.

I hate this. I hate him.

"Of course not. I'm happy, sweetheart. You know I am. I love you and the kids more than anything in this world. It was a mistake. One I regret more than you'll ever know."

Of course, I don't hate him at all.

"How long had it been going on?"

"I don't know. A few months. I haven't kept track. It was off and on."

"How many times did you sleep with her?"

"*What?*" he asks as if I've gone mad. Maybe I have.

"I need to know."

"Don't do this. How is knowing that going to help us?"

"It will help me a lot, actually. I need a number in my head."

He throws a hand in the air. "I don't know, Andi. I didn't tally it up."

"Five?" I press him. "Or more?"

He winces. "More, I think."

"More than a dozen?"

He nods.

"Twenty? Thirty?"

"Around that, I guess, yeah."

"Which? Twenty or thirty?"

He's silent. As if his silence could save us.

"*Spencer.*"

"Thirty or so, yeah."

"Where?"

"*Where?*"

"Where did you have sex with her?" I demand. "At work? In hotels? At her place? At *ours?*"

His chin drops to his chest. "At parties, mostly. Or hotels when I'd visit New York. Is this really necessary?"

I ignore the question. It's time he answered mine. "At parties? Like...in a closet?"

"Bedrooms," he says.

"And hotels?"

"Yes."

"Anywhere else? Here?"

"Never here," he assures me. As if that makes this better somehow.

"Her place?"

"No. Never."

I nod, batting back fresh tears. My chin quivers, betraying how strong I'm trying to appear.

"She means nothing to me," he tells me again, reaching for my cheek. "Nothing."

I pull away. "You've made that clear. How did it start?"

"Start?"

"Yes. What happened? Who made the first move? How did we get here, Spencer? I need you to tell me."

CHAPTER FOURTEEN

SPENCER

TWO YEARS AGO

Every time I come to New York City, I swear I'll never come back. And yet again, here I find myself, breathing in the unique scent combination of piss, garbage, and body odor that overwhelms the city.

I cross the street from my hotel, nearly getting plowed into by a taxi—whose horn honks like I'm the one who did something wrong—and dart into the restaurant. The second I enter, my phone goes off.

"Linda?"

"Spencer," she sings. She's joyous after the meeting we just had. "What time did you schedule the car for?"

"Six thirty. I sent you the confirmation and the company's phone number."

"Oh, I must've missed it. Where are you at? It sounds busy."

"I'm at the restaurant across the street grabbing a bite to

eat before I look over the new contracts." She hadn't bothered to invite me out to dinner with our new client—the reason for our trip and her exceptional mood.

"Excellent. Today went well, don't you think?"

"Yeah, you were great. Trent seems ecstatic."

"I'm going to change his life," she says simply. And it's true. Linda is one of the best. "He *should* be ecstatic."

Someday, when I'm an agent myself, I'll get to experience this sort of exuberant high firsthand. Even from where I sit, way, *way* down the ladder, it's hard not to be thrilled when we sign someone with so much potential. And Linda's right. As an agent, you do get to change people's lives—good people. People you care about. There's a sort of selflessness that comes with the job that excites me. We're making people's dreams come true. What could be better than that?

Not that it's entirely selfless. The money isn't bad, and the job itself comes with unending perks like exclusive parties with celebrities and the wealthiest people in the world, as well as plenty of business trips with *very little business* to do. For the most part, Linda uses our trips as an excuse to try out spas across the world. The assistants do most of the real work behind the scenes.

Speaking of...

"Anyway, be sure to let Stewart know we signed him. I'll see you at seven a.m. sharp," she says, interrupting my thoughts. "You scheduled a car to the airport, right?"

"Yep. I did. See you then."

"Goodbye."

I end the call and step forward toward the hostess waiting impatiently.

"How many?" she asks, not making eye contact, tapping

her way-too-long pink fingernails against the iPad in her hands.

"Just one."

"It's going to be an hour wait. Unless you want to sit at the bar." She juts a thumb over her shoulder. *Seriously, how does she not take out an eye with those things?*

I look ahead at the bar, which is mostly empty, except for an older couple lost in conversation and a heavyset man watching the football game on the TV above the bartender's head.

"Sure. Bar's fine."

She hands me a menu and waves her hand in that direction. I cross the crowded room, spying a fourth person sitting at the bar. A woman. She'd been hidden by the football-watching man.

I can't see her face, but I don't resist studying her body. Her long, dark-blonde hair goes down to her midback in soft waves. Her figure is...wow. I want to reach out and touch her, inspect every long line, every curve, every angle.

The woman's a knockout.

I take the seat next to her, planning to pretend it wasn't on purpose if she tells me to go away. To my relief, she doesn't.

Instead, she turns to look at me with a casual smile.

Damn.

Big blue-green eyes peek out at me from behind long dark lashes. There's something oddly familiar about her, but I can't put my finger on it. She looks young. Midtwenties, I'd guess. God, she's stunning. She runs her teeth over her bottom lip, which is a bright shade of red.

"Hi." When she speaks, her voice sends electricity

through me. It's soft and smooth, with a bit of rasp that nearly brings me to my knees.

God, I've been away from home too long.

"Hi."

She leans forward, swirling the straw in the half-empty red cocktail she's drinking.

"Can I buy you another?" I ask.

"I would love that. Thank you."

I wave the bartender over and order a whiskey for myself and another of whatever she's having. Something with more sugar than alcohol. The bartender sets to work, allowing me to return my attention to her.

"Are you...here with someone?"

"In New York? Or here at this restaurant?"

"Either. Both."

"I'm here visiting friends. Considering moving here permanently. But I'm at this restaurant alone." She smiles with one side of her mouth. "At least, I was."

I extend my hand. "I'm Spencer."

She takes it, shaking it slowly. "Spencer. I like that."

The bartender returns and slides us both our drinks, then asks if I want to start a tab. I hand him my card and ask to settle up for the drinks instead. "I'm here for work. Can't stay too long."

She nods. "That's too bad. What do you do?"

"I'm a talent agent," I say. It's just a minor lie, really. Insignificant. I *will* be a talent agent. Someday. "In town to sign a new client."

Her eyes brighten. "What a coincidence." She wiggles her shoulders, giving me a confident smile. "I'm trying to get into acting."

"You certainly look the part," I say, then clear my throat. "I'm an agent for musicians, though. I could get you the information for one of my colleagues that works with actresses."

"That would be amazing, Spencer. Thank you."

"Anytime... Actually, I didn't get your name."

"It's... Well, now that you mention it, I'm trying out some stage names. What do you think of Anna?"

"Hmm..." I pretend to think. Truth is, this girl could call herself Igor and I'm still sure she'll be a star. There are a lot of beautiful women out there, but there's something special about this one. I feel it in my gut.

...and maybe a bit lower.

I'd like to think it's the agent's intuition kicking in, but who knows? What I do know is that I've never cheated on my wife, though I've been given plenty of opportunities to do just that. I've never had any desire to until this moment.

"Anna is nice. Not quite special enough for you."

Pink flushes her cheeks. "What would you suggest, then?"

"Where are you from?"

"Nashville," she says, and I detect the first hint of an accent coming through in her speech, *Nash-vull*, not *Nash-ville*. It's slight, hardly noticeable. "And please don't tell me I should call myself Loretta or Dolly."

Shit. She's from Nashville. It hits me all at once. I blanch.

"I'm joking," she says when her comment doesn't land how she'd expected it to.

"No, I know. It's just..." I don't want to tell her. Telling her could bring me a world of trouble. Then again, if I actually want to help her with her acting career, this could be my chance. It doesn't have to have anything to do with my attraction to her or desire to see her again. I can be selfless. "I'm also from Nashville."

Her dark brows draw down. "You're kidding."

I wish I was. "Nope. Born and raised."

"Me too. What are the odds? Some of the only born-and-raised Nashvillians left in the world, and we meet in a New York City bar." She laughs.

I start to tell her that's where my agency is. I really do want to be selfless, to offer to call in favors, but before I can say anything, I realize if she were to ever come in, she'd know I lied.

Instead, I say, "You don't have much of an accent."

She rolls her eyes playfully. "That's on purpose. I hate my accent. It mostly only comes out when I'm drinking or sleepy."

I laugh. "Okay. Hmm. What about Presley? For a name. It's unique. Hearkens back to your Tennessee roots without being on the nose. You could say your mom was a huge fan of Elvis. People would think it was sweet."

"Hearkens, hmm? So fancy."

I chuckle, my cheeks burning.

"Presley." She thinks it over, her head tilting back and forth. "It has a nice ring to it, yeah." Taking another sip of her drink, she sits up straighter. "Tell you what"—she presses her tongue to her top teeth, a devilish look in her eyes—"you call me Presley tonight, and I'll see what I think of it."

I have no idea if she meant that the way I heard it. I adjust in my seat to keep from showing the entire restaurant exactly how I took it.

"I can do that."

"Excellent." She wraps her lips around the straw in front of her, and it's impossible not to picture those red lips wrapped around something else entirely.

I swallow. "Would you...like to have dinner? With me?"

TWO HOURS LATER, we leave the bar. I've had four drinks, which is well above the limit I usually set for myself, but I need liquid courage if I'm going to go through with my plan.

If I'm going to become a cheater.

An adulterer.

Everything that happens from this point on will draw a line in the sand. Before the affair—before I crossed this invisible line. And after.

With a single decision, over the course of a few short hours, I am becoming who I swore I'd never be, and yet I can't seem to stop myself from moving forward. I could call this off at any time. I could wish her good night, help her catch a cab, and never see her again.

But I don't.

It's as simple as that.

I could tell her I'm married, but I don't.

I could stop her from coming up to my hotel room, but I don't.

I could tell her I should call it a night, but I don't.

I could stop myself from leaning in for a kiss once we're safely inside my room, from breathing her in. Running my hands through her hair. I could stop myself from pulling the shirt over her head, from cupping her breasts, kissing them, biting. I could stop myself from allowing her lips to trail my stomach, to go even lower. Stop her from unbuckling my pants, placing me in her mouth.

But I don't.

I don't.

I don't.

I don't.

With those eyes staring up at me, those pretty lips gliding back and forth, I'm a goner.

Without wasting a single thought on it, I cross the line I swore I never would. And, minutes later, when I'm sinking deep inside a woman who isn't my wife, hearing her cry my name, feeling her body tighten and react to my every move, I know I'll never look back.

More than that, I'm sure I'll never want to.

CHAPTER FIFTEEN

ANDI

After Spencer tells me the story of how he met Heidi for the first time, I have to walk away. There are no words to describe how badly he's hurt me, how betrayed I feel.

I thought somehow that we were immune to this. That we were above all the couples who succumb to desiring other people. To acting on those desires.

We weren't like those people.

We were better.

Stronger.

More in love.

Is that what they all thought, too?

Our marriage has always been so stable. Never faltering. We don't have blow-up fights. After ten years, he's never once slept on the couch. We're happy.

I was happy.

I've never had any reason to suspect he wasn't.

To settle myself down, I slip into bed and flip off the lamp. Then, I call Jo.

I can hear the kids in the background when she answers, and I can't help missing them. It's Spencer's fault they can't be here, and that makes me hate him more.

Do I hate him?

Right now, yes, I do.

But I also love him.

Life is complicated.

"Hey! How's Spencer feeling?"

"Still under the weather. He's sleeping. I just wanted to call and check in with the kids before bed. How are they doing?"

"Great. We're watching the new *Matilda* and eating popcorn. I brought home pizza for dinner, but apparently James doesn't like sausage anymore, so he had chicken nuggets instead." She chuckles.

"Oh, that's right. The sausage thing is new. He informed us the other morning at breakfast. Sorry about that. I told you he's going through a picky phase."

"No trouble. I bought approximately a mountain of food to get through the weekend, so it worked out. More pizza for me and Ava, isn't that right?"

"Yeah!" Ava shrieks in the background.

"A mountain, hmm?" I laugh. I miss them so much it physically hurts. Something I've never heard anyone else talk about as a parent, but I've found true for me, is that our kids make me feel safe. When I'm away from my kids for too long, I find myself on edge. Even when I'm enjoying myself, I always think I'd enjoy it a bit more if they were home.

I know they're safe with Jo, but that doesn't stop me from

wishing they could be here with me.

"Do they want to talk?"

"Kids, your mom wants to say hi before bed."

"Hi!" James calls from what sounds like across the room.

"Not now. This is the good part!" Ava says.

"Sorry, they're preoccupied. Want me to pause the movie?"

I sigh. "No, that's okay. Let them have fun. What are your plans for tomorrow?"

"We haven't decided yet. We talked about the zoo or the botanical garden."

"The kids love Cheekwood," I say, thinking back over the many memories we have there—Christmas lights in December, pumpkins in the fall, and the different seasonal plants in bloom throughout spring and summer. Now, all the memories are tainted by what Spencer has done. Will it always be that way? Will I ever trust him again? Ever feel safe with him again?

I just want this to end.

"Yeah. James wants to go to Opry Mills, but I'm trying to find something else to do. Last time I went on a Saturday, I swore I never would again."

"It's a nightmare. You know you don't have to take them anywhere. They're more than happy to just hang around the house with you."

"I have a reputation to uphold," she says playfully. "Aunt Jo is the fun aunt."

"You're right about that. I'm glad they're having a good time."

"You sound sad... Is everything okay?"

"Yeah, of course. I just miss them."

"They miss you, too, but try not to be sad. Catch up on some trashy TV, sleep in, eat junk food in your pajamas all day. Enjoy the weekend. It's just two days."

I run a hand over my face. "You're right. I know you are."

"Of course I am."

The bedroom door opens. Spencer is standing there, phone to his ear. "Yes, but I really think you're overreacting." He waves a hand at me.

I put a hand over the speaker, shooing him away. "Hey, Jo, I've gotta go. I'll call you in the morning."

"Not too early," she warns. "I mean, I'll be awake, but one of us should get to sleep in. I expect you to get a full night's sleep."

Still in the doorway, Spencer waves his arm again, this time frantically, trying to get my attention. I wave back at him. *Just a minute.*

"Promise," I say. "Good night."

"'Night."

Spencer comes to stand next to the bed and flips on the lamp. He puts his phone on speaker, but I only hear half of the sentence being said.

"—eck in with the rental company to see where her car was left. It was supposed to be returned this evening. Evelyn's planning to call the police to report it stolen."

Her car.

The words slam into my chest like a wall of bricks, and I finally understand the terrified look on my husband's face.

"Can she even do that?" he asks.

"Apparently," the man on the phone says.

"Right. Well, it's still early. Just seven. Maybe Heidi's just late with it."

"Maybe, but Evelyn says this isn't like her. She worked hard to get the role she had just accepted. To throw it all away without talking to anyone is hard for her to grasp. It has everyone pretty worried. I spoke with Sarah, and even she agreed this isn't normal."

"Right. Yeah, it's hard to say," Spencer mumbles. I have no idea what he's talking about, and by the dazed look on his face, neither does he.

"Anyway, Evelyn is planning to contact the rental car company in just a few minutes to see about using GPS to locate it. They told her earlier they'll automatically report it as stolen and give the location to the police if it hasn't been returned by morning, but that was before the five o'clock cutoff time. She thinks she can get them to check it sooner if it's still not been returned. I just wanted to touch base in case you'd heard from her before she calls them again."

"No." Spencer pats his cheek rhythmically. "No, man, I haven't. I'll let you know if I do. I'm sure it's fine."

"Let's hope so. Thanks for keeping an eye out. I'll let you know what we find out."

"Cool. Thanks."

When the call ends, I ask the question I'm terrified to get an answer to. "They're going to track her car?"

He nods. "I don't know why I never thought about how she got here. She just showed up. She was only in town for a day. I assumed she took an Uber and wanted me to give her a ride back to her hotel."

I had assumed Spencer picked her up from her hotel and brought her here, but now that I think about it, that makes very little sense. Then again, it's not as if I've had much time to think at all today.

I rub my temple, my blood pressure rising. "But...there are no cars in the driveway. Where else would it be?"

He chews the inside of his lip, not answering.

"Spence, look at me." I place my hands on his chest.

We're going to lose the kids. This is all over. Terror swims through my veins, but I can't break down. I have to make him see reason, even if it kills me to do so.

"Look at me. Please. Listen, I know it's not what you want to hear, but if they track her car and find out it's at our house, we're done for. That's it. It's all over. *And, even if we can somehow locate it*"—I head off his argument—"you already got rid of her purse and keys. We'll have no way to move it, not to mention no time." The words taste bitter on my tongue.

After all we've gone through, to give up feels like a loss and a relief at the same time. "Maybe we should let her go. Turn yourself in and tell them what happened. We haven't hurt her yet. Not really. She's still alive. It's not too late."

To my surprise, he doesn't look angry at the suggestion. Instead, he cocks a brow.

"What is it?"

"Don't get mad, but you just gave me an idea."

"What idea?" Is he going to suggest a reconciliation between the two of them? Is he going to leave me to maintain our secret? What will I do if he does? Is that what I want? I honestly don't know anymore.

I just want to wake up and find out this entire day never happened.

"We need to find her car and move it."

"Yes, but we can't because—"

"We can. I still have her keys."

CHAPTER SIXTEEN

SPENCER

We don't have much time.

I have no idea how long it'll take us to find her car, no idea how soon the police will try to locate it if it's reported stolen tonight, and no idea how quickly they'll be able to track her car if they do look into it.

In the kitchen, I reach into the trash can and remove the fast-food bag from earlier, silently thanking the cop who walked past and terrified me so much I couldn't throw her things out.

If I had, we'd officially be screwed.

Andi is always telling me I'm one of the luckiest people she knows. I guess I managed to find a small bit of luck after all.

I tear the bag open, retrieving Heidi's purse and phone.

"You were supposed to get rid of those," Andi says in utter shock, her voice weak.

I don't have time to argue or explain. "Be glad I didn't."

With Heidi's possessions in my hand, I grab the keys to

Andi's car and head for the door. As I walk, I dig through the tiny purse in search of a set of keys. It doesn't take me long to find them. "I'll leave my phone here, but you take yours."

"Why? What's your plan?"

"I want you to take our car and wait for me at the pharmacy near the extra airport parking on the corner of Donelson and Elm Hill. I'll take her car and drop it off in a hotel parking lot. Go a different route than I do. I'll leave the keys, her purse, and phone inside it. Doors unlocked. Hopefully, someone will take it and help us muddy the waters a bit. Then, I'll come find you. With my phone still here, if anyone were to look into it, it would look like you were getting medicine for me and I was still home sick."

"How are you going to find her car?"

"Well, I'm hoping..." I open the door, peering out into the dark street, and press the alarm button. Within seconds, I hear an alarm in the distance. "There it is." To my surprise, the flashing hazard lights come from the small, black car parked on the street in front of the house directly across from us.

"She parked across the street," Andi whispers.

I hand her the keys and hurry forward. "Take the interstate to get there, okay? Be safe. I'll swing through the subdivision and take back roads."

I unlock the rental car with Heidi's keys, hoping we'll have enough time to get it somewhere without the company or the police locating it. A hotel near the airport feels like the safest bet to continue the lie we're trying to sell.

I wrap my hands around the steering wheel, feeling nauseous.

We're so close, but things keep popping up at every turn. Like the universe is conspiring against us.

It was never meant to go this way.

That first night two years ago, I never dreamed I could ever live to regret what I'd done. Now, the joke's on me.

Nothing is worth this. Nothing at all.

It only takes about ten minutes for me to find a hotel that looks like cars could easily go missing from it. I park the rental car and use the sleeve of my shirt to wipe down the steering wheel, gearshift, and seat.

It's not perfect. I should do it better, but I'm working with what I have. I toss her purse and phone into the passenger seat, place the keys on the dash, and shut the door.

Then, I shove my hands in my pocket and walk away from it, at peace with my decision.

No one asks any questions as I go. The people I pass have no reason to be suspicious of me. I look like a normal person. A loving father. A doting husband. I don't look like a murderer.

That's exactly why I'll get away with this.

IT'S A LONGER WALK to the pharmacy than the drive took, and when I finally see it come into view, I worry for half a second that Andi may have left me stranded.

I wouldn't blame her, truth be told. What I've done, what I've put her through, is unforgivable.

I know that—I'm not a monster.

I fully recognize that this isn't okay.

Once again, I find myself at a point where I fully recognize that I could stop things before we go any further.

The last time I refused to stop—against my better judgment—it was for my own selfish desire. This time, I won't stop because of Andi. I can't bear the thought of putting her through this. If I were to go to jail, it would ruin her.

She can't do this alone.

She needs me.

As selfish, as foolish, as terrible as I am, she needs me, and I can't let her suffer because of what I've done. As soon as Heidi is taken care of, I'll be better. I know I will. I've learned my lesson the hard way, but I've learned it nonetheless.

As I approach our car and my exhausted-looking wife sitting in the driver's seat, I know I'm a changed man.

CHAPTER SEVENTEEN

ANDI

This isn't normal.

I know this, and yet, I'm carrying on. I picture those memes on social media—mindless encouragement to keep calm and carry on. Would they still implore me to do that if they knew what I was carrying on to do?

Perhaps the last thing I should be doing is *carrying on.*

Perhaps I should call it all off.

Would he lock me in the basement then, too?

Try as I might, I still can't reconcile this version of my husband with who I know him to be. It's a problem I've had all day. On the one hand, he's the man who never ever yells at me, who never loses his temper, who went out and got me whatever I was craving when I was pregnant without complaint, who rubs my feet after hard days and never has to be asked to pick up his dirty clothes.

How can that be the same man sitting next to me? How can any of this be real? How can he be okay with what's coming next?

With murder?

How could he so easily have come up with a plan—with so many plans—of how best to do this?

We'll never be the same after this.

MY THOUGHTS COME IN FRAGMENTS.

Sometimes, there's nothing at all. Sometimes, I'm completely numb, as if my mind has shut off to prevent me from seeing what I'm about to.

Other times, it races. With panic and worry. With regret. With insistent ideas about how to get out of this. With urges to turn him in.

With urges to walk away from it all.

Spencer is mostly silent too, staring out the passenger window as we drive home. At one point, he leans down and lifts the plastic bag from between his feet with one finger before digging inside it.

"What's this?"

"Medicine."

He pulls out the bottle of nausea medicine I purchased while waiting for him at the pharmacy.

"To make the story more solid. In case... In case anyone asks why I went."

"Smart thinking." He puts the bottle back into the bag and drops it to the floor.

No. If I was smart, I wouldn't be in this mess.

NOW THAT I'VE had more time to process everything that's happened over the last few hours, I keep thinking back to the way Heidi looked down there in the basement. Yes, she's being vile. Yes, she's disgusting and cruel and a home-wrecker who tried to ruin my family, but she was right about something. She's still a woman. If it were me, if it were Ava, I would count on—hope and pray for—a woman to step up and say something. Women who look the other way, who don't believe other women, who accuse and torment and tease, who tear other women down in order to make them-selves look or feel better...they're the real enemies.

Not men.

Men are the obvious enemies.

We know they're dangerous.

It's when other women betray us that we can be hurt the most. We expect pain from men—expect them to abuse and assault, to rape and annihilate us. It's what we've been warned about since we were little girls.

Don't smile at strange men, but also don't be rude. It could get you killed. Don't accept rides from strangers. Don't hurt his feelings. Keep your keys between your fingers when you walk to your car. Always check your back seat before getting in. Don't dress a certain way. Don't go on dates unless you've told people where you'll be and whom you're with. Watch your drink at all times. Don't tell them where you live. Don't bring them around your kids. Look the other way when they make inappropriate comments. When they touch you. When they do even more.

"Boys will be boys" turns into men who will be men, and our only protection in this world is the belief and support of other women.

We are all we have in this world—to speak up for each other, to fight for each other, to believe each other—because, at the end of the day, even *good* men are capable of atrocities.

I thought I'd found an exception. One of the good ones. But I should've known better. Even my dad, as good a dad as he is—and he *is* good—lost his temper, punched walls, belittled us when he was angry. By finding someone so calm, so unlike him, I thought I'd broken the cycle. I'd purposefully searched for someone who is the opposite of my trauma, and yet, here we are.

It's always the quiet ones.

I made the mistake once before, so I guess I should've known.

I was fifteen at the time. He was a friend of a friend whom I'd connected with online. These were the days of chatrooms and instant messaging, but my friends all knew him. I thought because I was following the rules, because he wasn't a total stranger, I would be safe.

I thought he liked me.

I snuck out that night to meet him, still in shock that someone like him, someone twenty-one and in a band, would be interested in someone like me.

We'd been talking online for a few days, and he was getting frustrated that I couldn't go out with him. In truth, I never asked, but I knew what the answer would be. He was too old for me. My parents would never allow it.

I thought I knew better than they did.

Scared I was going to lose his interest, I finally agreed to meet him one night. The catch was that it had to be late. I had to sneak out. He parked in a field near my house, and I walked to him. To this day, I can still remember the buzz of adrenaline when I saw him for the first time. He was handsome and funny and *so cool*.

We'd been there for less than half an hour when he asked me to get into the back seat with him. I liked him, so I went. Why would I say no? I thought we were just going to make out for a while, and I desperately wanted that. We'd just met; I never thought he'd want more so quickly. More than that, I still thought I was safe with him. He knew friends of mine, friends who considered him a friend. They'd never put me in danger.

But I was wrong.

I told him no.

I told him my parents might wake up and realize I was gone.

I told him I should get back home.

I told him no.

His response? "You don't think I drove all this way just to kiss you, do you?"

I wasn't a virgin at that point, but the two boys I'd slept with were boyfriends I cared about. When I told him I hardly knew him, he said I shouldn't have asked him to come there.

He was angry with me then. I could see it in his eyes, hear it in his voice when he claimed I was wasting his time.

He still wasn't opening the door for me to get out or offering a ride home. When I moved to reach for the door, he lifted me up and placed me on his lap.

He pressed his mouth to mine. Hard.

I tasted blood. I'm still not sure if it was his or mine.

From there, I froze. I didn't know what else to do. He was older. Bigger. I was in his car, where I wasn't supposed to be. If my parents found out I'd snuck out, I wasn't sure what would happen. There was a big party coming up, and I didn't want to be grounded. More than that, I was scared he would hurt me, hold me down and force me if I didn't give in. If I fought, I might make it worse.

So, I didn't.

I gave him what he wanted, what he felt he deserved.

It was over fast—that was the one merciful thing. When he was done with me, he let me out of the car and drove away with a brief kiss on the lips and the quiet sentiment, "Nice ass."

I didn't cry. I was numb.

In no way did I consider what had happened to me to be rape.

I'd given in. I hadn't fought him. He didn't have to hold me down. He didn't hurt me. There were no bruises.

If anything, it was some sort of *rape lite* situation—*rape-ish, rape-like*, maybe, but not rape—and to ever tell anyone would mean admitting to my parents I'd snuck out of the house to meet an older man in the first place. At fifteen, that felt like a fate worse than death. Besides, it was my own fault, wasn't it? What did I think was going to happen? Why else did I think he was meeting me in the middle of the night? I'd been too young, too naive to know better, but that wasn't his fault. It was mine.

In college, after years of it weighing on me, Jo was the first person I ever told about that night. She was honest with me about what happened—I'd said no, and he hadn't listened. Whatever I called it, it wasn't okay. It wasn't right. It wasn't my fault.

When I told my boyfriend at the time next, expecting support, expecting him to confirm what Jo said, he told me it was a gray area. He asked if I "made noises and stuff" and said if I seemed like I was into it, maybe the guy just thought I was trying not to seem too easy or wanted to play hard to get. That he was sorry it happened, but it sounded like I gave in eventually. How was the guy supposed to know I was actually saying no? *How could he have known?*

I never told anyone else.

WHEN WE PULL up to the house, I'm still thinking about that night. The conversations that followed.

I wish so badly I'd had someone before Jo to tell me it wasn't my fault. That he'd been wrong. That I never owed him my body in exchange for his time. I wish I'd been strong enough to get out of that car.

Then again, if I'd tried, would it have been worse? Would he have killed me?

The thoughts and worries that have haunted me over the years about that night are back as I shove the bag from the pharmacy into my purse. We walk into the house without a word, and Spencer pulls out a few trash bags from under the sink.

"The tarp's in the garage," he says with a deep breath. "I'm going to get it and then we'll be ready." He pauses, studying me. "I've been thinking...maybe you should stay up here."

I cock my head to the side. Can he sense what I'm think-ing? Does he know I'm hesitating?

"You were right earlier. You shouldn't have to do this. It's my mess. I should clean it up."

It. She's an it now. A mess to clean.

The woman in my basement was my husband's lover, a woman he must've cared about in some way, and now her life is going to end unless I do something to save her.

I nod, watching him walk away.

Twenty years ago, if I'd fought back, could I have been Heidi? Different situations, but could I have been the girl to die at the hand of someone I trusted?

Could I still?

I have a choice—her or him.

My marriage or my soul.

I close my eyes, steeling myself as I drag in a long inhale.

I'm sorry.

Decision made, I grab a knife from the block on the counter and turn away from the kitchen island. I grab a chair from the dinner table, tiptoeing toward the basement door. Pushing it open, I step inside, easing it shut and wedging a chair against it. I tug at the doorknob, making sure it's secure.

It won't hold for long, but it's the only option.

Funny how that phrase seems to be haunting me lately.

I flip on the light and tiptoe down the stairs.

When she sees me, her eyes narrow. He's placed a new piece of tape over her mouth. I step forward, tearing it off without warning.

She winces, sucking in a sharp breath through clenched teeth, then flicks a glance at the knife. "What are you plan-ning to do with that?"

"We don't have much time. I need to ask you something."

"I've got nothing but time. Unless you're planning to kill me right now." She rests her head against the post behind her.

"I'm not going to kill you." I shove the knife into my pocket. If she says yes to this question, my decision will be made. "I need you to tell me something. Did Spencer ever hurt you? Before today? Did he ever hit you or...or touch you when you didn't want him to?"

Her upper lip curls. "No. Why?"

My hope fades. "Never? You swear it?"

"Why would I lie? Why are you asking this?" Her gaze falters. "Wait...does he hurt you?"

"No." The word is a whisper. "He's not this man. I know you had to see that. He's kind and tender. I want you to remember that when I let you go. I want you to remember how good he was to you...when he was."

"How *good* he was to me?" she asks, eyes searching the room as if I'm pranking her. "Is that a joke? What are you talking about?"

I stare at her, my head growing fuzzy. "Come on, for you to be having an affair with him for months now, it can't have all been bad. I'm going to let you go, but I just need you to promise me you'll think about—"

"Wait a second. *An affair?*" She laughs. Loudly. As if it's the most ridiculous thing she's ever heard. "Are you kidding me? Who told you we were having an affair?"

Upstairs, Spencer is in the kitchen. I hear him call my name; I ignore him.

"It was an affair. I know you were just sleeping together,

not in a relationship, but whatever you call it, he was married to me the whole time."

She twists her lips, studying me as if she's just worked something out. "Andi... You have no idea why he has me down here, do you?"

CHAPTER EIGHTEEN

ANDI

The floor seems to shift underneath me at her words. "What are you talking about?" I demand. "Of course I do."

Spencer is banging on the door upstairs now, obviously having worked out that I'm down here.

"*Andi, let me in!* The door is stuck. Are you okay?"

In front of me, Heidi shakes her head slowly. "I wasn't sleeping with your husband, Andi."

Her words are like darts, stabbing holes in the shell of my reality. Everything begins to blur. She's lying...but why? Why would she lie? Why now?

"You were."

"*Andi!*" he bellows. He's really pounding on the door now.

"I wasn't. No offense, but he's not my type."

I squeeze my eyes shut, trying to drown out the noise Spencer is making so I can focus on what she's saying. "If you're just lying to get me to let you go, don't bother. I've already made up my mind. I can't do this. I told you I'm going to let you go and hope you do the right thing... Whatever that is." Truth is, I don't even know anymore. There are no villains or heroes in this story. We've all done bad things.

"Andi, listen to me." Her tone is urgent now. "I knew your husband when I was in school, but I hadn't seen him again until today."

"What are you talking about?"

"He told you we were having an affair?"

I nod.

"*Andi!*" Spencer shouts. "What the hell is going on? *Please! Let me in!* You're scaring me!"

A distant look comes over her eyes. "All this time, I thought you were just some heartless monster. You said the thing about telling your daughter not to sleep with married men." She swallows as her gaze focuses on me once again. "But... I'm just realizing you were talking about me."

"Who else would I be talking about?"

She blinks. "*My* daughter."

I hardly hear her over the sound of Spencer's banging upstairs, which has become incessant. Feral.

"*What?*"

CRACK. CRACK. CRACK.

He's pounding something hard against the door. I can hear the wood splintering from where I stand. It's only a matter of time until he breaks through.

"She's only seventeen, Andi."

My stomach clenches. "What are you talking about?"

"They met at a bar when she was spending the summer

with me in New York. She had a fake ID I got her so she could go to bars. I thought it was innocent fun. Something I would've done when I was her age. She was always such a good kid. She promised me she'd just have one drink." She shakes her head.

"*Andi!*"

I cover the ear that's closest to the door with my hand, struggling to focus on what she's telling me. It's impossible. Why is she lying?

"I know how that must make me sound, but we never had the best relationship. I had her when I was really young. I was trying to become an actress, and I'd just moved to L.A. to pursue acting. I came back home to visit my folks and hooked up with an ex. It was one night, and my entire future flashed before my eyes. Everything I'd worked for... I wasn't ready to be a mom. Maybe you can't understand that. Her father couldn't."

She looks away. "But he took her in. He was good to her. Raised her on his own. I tried to stay in touch, to visit when I could, but my life was a mess back then. When things got steadier for me, when I settled down in New York, I realized how much I was missing out on. She was a teenager at that point. I just... I wanted her to like me. I just wanted to be the cool mom. I trusted her to make better decisions than I did."

THUD.

CRACK. CRACK.

"*Andi!*"

I press a fist to my lips, trying to steady my breathing. "You're telling me that your *seventeen-year-old* daughter slept with my husband?"

She presses her lips together. "She told me about it yesterday, and I forced her to tell me who he was. When she said his name and I realized I knew him, I flew down to confront him. Clearly, I wasn't thinking straight. I was just so angry. I told him I was going to the police, that I had pictures and videos he'd sent her and screenshots of their conversations. I wanted to know if he knew her age. I needed to look him in the eye when I asked, to see the truth for myself. He was always so quiet in school... I never thought he'd try to hurt me."

"You said he didn't hurt you," I point out.

"The fall may have been an accident, but he'd already made it clear he wasn't planning to let me tell anyone."

"*Andi! For Christ's sake, let me in!*" CRACK. CRACK. CRACK.

I feel as if I might pass out. I'm a teacher, for crying out loud, and my husband is a...a what? A pedophile? A statutory rapist? I can see the headlines now.

"You said you..." I press a hand to my stomach. I'm going to pass out. I can't breathe. How does it just keep getting worse? "You wanted to know if he knew how old she was. Did he?" I ask.

CRACK.

Before she can answer, there's a loud splintering sound, followed by a bang. My husband's footsteps descend the stairs.

He's coming.

We're too late.

I hurry around behind her and cut the tape off her wrists with my knife, then slide it back into my pocket. She jiggles her arms as if she's surprised to be free.

"What did you do, Andi?" When I look up, Spencer is standing at the bottom of the stairs, a pistol in his hand.

"Is it true?" I ask, my vision blurring with rage.

"Is *what* true?" He scowls. "You can't believe anything she says. She's an actress. She'll do anything to be with me. She's in love with me, Andi. You know that."

"Is it true that you slept with her daughter? With a teenager?"

He lowers the gun slightly, shaking his head. I expect him to deny it. To call her a liar. Instead, he says, "I'm so sorry. It was a mistake. I didn't know how old she was. We met in a bar. She was drinking. I assumed she was twenty-one."

"So, the affair wasn't with Heidi, then? It's her daughter you slept with? You lied to me about everything?"

He swallows. "It was a mistake. I didn't know what else to do."

"Why not just tell me the truth?" I demand. "You were confessing anyway."

"Because I didn't want you to look at me the way you're looking at me right now. An affair is one thing, and that was hard enough to admit, but I couldn't tell you everything. You'd never forgive me. At least the other way, I thought I had a chance. It was an accident... Did she lie to you about that?" He waves the gun in her direction. "I never pushed her. I was only trying to get her to listen to me. To listen to reason."

Behind me, Heidi is still trying to stand, her legs obviously asleep and sore. I can't take my eyes off Spencer.

"Yes, she told me it was an accident. I believe you. I just wish you'd told me the truth from the beginning."

"Would it have mattered? Whether I told you the truth or a lie? You weren't supposed to talk to her. I thought I was sparing you." His expression wrinkles. "I hate myself for what I did. You have to believe me."

"You really didn't know her age?"

He shakes his head. "Honest. I never would've gone through with it if I did." When he steps forward, I don't budge, trying to make sense of it all in my head.

"We have to let her go, Spence. She's a mother protecting her child. Would we have done anything differently if the situation had been reversed? If it was Ava? Or James?"

He's quiet for a moment, watching me. Finally, he drops the gun to his side. "You're right. I know you're right. I'm just... I'm terrified. I don't know what will happen to me."

"I know. I'm scared, too."

He steps forward again, arms held out. "Can you just tell me this much... Will you ever forgive me?"

"It will be easier to forgive if you let her go," I vow. It's the only thing I can promise right now.

With another step, he's in front of me. He holds his arms out, ready to gather me into a hug. At his surrender, I feel a sense of calm spread through me. There is so much unknown, but if I can save her, everything else will be okay. It's all I know, but for now, it's enough.

I fall into his arms, breathing in the scent of him. I'm numb again. Lost and confused and so utterly exhausted.

BANG.

I jolt as the gunshot rings out. He squeezes me tighter, trying to prevent me from pulling away. His hot breath is on my ear as I shake my head.

No.

"I'm sorry." His voice is barely above a whisper, only meant for me to hear.

The smell hits me first. An acrid bite to the air. Blood.

I know she's gone before I see her, but when he finally releases me, I turn around. I regret it instantly. I was wrong. She's still alive, but just barely.

No.

She clutches her stomach and her chest with trembling hands. It's impossible to tell where the blood is coming from as the dark stain engulfs her shirt. Sticky, red blood coats her fingers as she tries to make sense of what's happened.

No.

When she looks up, she opens her mouth to say something, meeting my eyes and lifting a hand to reach for me.

You failed, I bet she's thinking. *This is your fault.*

I'm so sorry. I want to go to her, but Spencer keeps a firm grip on my hand. He won't let me leave. I'm a fifteen-year-old girl in the back seat of that car again. Trapped.

It's a different man, but it's not all that different.

If I try to run, he might kill me.

So, I stay. I stand still and watch as she dies in front of us. Doing nothing. There's nothing to be done.

She closes her mouth and opens it again, and I watch in pure, frozen horror as blood drips out over her lips, down her chin. She doesn't seem to realize it's happening.

I cover my own mouth with my free hand, knowing I'm going to be sick, and turn away. He releases my hand as I begin to vomit, then doesn't try to stop me as I rush away from him.

Before I make it too far, I lean over my knees, spewing

the day's worth of stress, fear, and anger onto the concrete floor. I grip onto the side of a step for support.

When I'm finished, I stagger. I'm too weak to go. Too weak to fight.

I look up to find her still alive. Still watching me.

Seconds later, her eyes glaze over and she's gone.

CHAPTER NINETEEN

ANDI

I sit on the basement steps in a state of shock as my husband cleans up the blood with our good towels.

He's overexplaining. Telling me he had no other choice.

For the most part, I've tuned him out.

I can't breathe. Can't think. If any of the neighbors heard the gunshot, there's a chance they could've called the police. Then again, it's late and the shot came from the basement, so they may not have heard anything, and if they did, they couldn't be sure where the sound came from. And, of course, our subdivision backs up against several dozen acres of woods before it eventually reaches the lake, so it's not entirely unusual to hear gunshots here anyway.

But this late at night?

Maybe they'll think it was the Jensens' son's car backfiring again. I can't be sure. A few minutes pass with me sitting on the steps, trying to make sense of my new reality before I realize he's still talking.

"—never how it was supposed to go. I think you know

that. But I had to protect our family. I know what you must think of me, but this wasn't about me, Andi. If it was, I would've just gone to the police and turned myself in. Or let her turn me in. But I had to protect you. And the kids."

He tosses another bloody towel onto the pile, wiping sweat from his brow with his upper arm.

"I knew if we were caught, it would cost you everything. If the truth about the girl came out, they'd never let you be a teacher again. I couldn't live with myself if I was the one who cost you what you love."

He couldn't live with himself. And yet, Heidi's the one dead on the floor right now.

"Besides, it's not like this changes anything from a few hours ago. I told you about the affair. It was still an affair. Just because she was a teenager... I didn't know. You can't hold that against me."

"Of course not," I mutter, my lips too dry. "How could you have known?"

"Exactly. She tricked me. And then Heidi came here, accusing me of things, calling me all sorts of things that weren't true. I should've never slept with anyone else. I know that. I admit that and accept all responsibility for it."

Another towel, and still so much blood. Even with so much of it soaked into the comforter underneath her. She was tiny. How is there this much blood?

"I wasn't thinking straight that night. Linda and I had just signed Trent DeGrassi to the agency, and I was still riding that high a little bit. And, I mean, it's not an excuse, but she was just there, you know? I hadn't been home for a few weeks. I was lonely and... It doesn't matter anymore. She's been the only one, I swear it."

I'm slowly processing what he's saying, my heart pounding so hard in my ears I'm having to force myself to focus. "Wait..."

He stops scrubbing and looks up at me.

"You had just signed Trent when this happened? That was...that was years ago."

He hesitates. "It was two years ago, yeah. Heidi didn't tell you that?"

"Was the girl seventeen when you slept with her? Or is she seventeen now?"

He blanches. "How would I know? I..."

"You told me you'd slept with her thirty or so times, Spencer. Was that a lie? Or are you still sleeping with her?"

Hotels, he'd said. And parties. Never her house. Never his.

Was it all just a lie?

Or could he not sleep with her at her house because her parents would be home?

I'm going to be sick again.

He pushes up from the floor, a hand bouncing in the air to calm me down. "Andi, listen, it's over. It's over now. I'm done wi—"

I stand. "She was *fifteen* when you met her? When you slept with her?"

He opens his mouth but only manages to stutter. "I... I mean... It... Look—" A wheezing laugh escapes his throat.

"How could you not have known? She was a child, Spencer! *A child.* Did you ever know?"

"No." His laughter is nervous. He pinches the bridge of his nose, sliding his hand down. He doesn't seem to notice the smear of blood it leaves. "Of course not. I didn't know how old she was, okay? I thought she was young, yes, but not that young. I mean, look at her mom. Heidi is three years older than me and she still looks like she's twenty-one." His smile fades, and he shakes his head. "Please believe me. I never ever knew. I thought she was young, but she was in a bar."

"Did you ask how old she was?"

"She was in a bar," he repeats, his voice whiny, exasperated.

I look down, trying to catch my breath. Because she was in a bar, underage, she was asking for it. Maybe she was, I don't know. Maybe she was all too willing. Maybe he's telling me the truth, that he never knew she was fifteen, sixteen, or seventeen.

That she never mentioned school to him. Or her friends.

That he never got the sense she was lying about her age.

I want to believe my husband could be so clueless, but I can't.

"Come here." He takes another step forward, his shoes tracking through her blood. His arms are outstretched, waiting for me. Waiting for me to say it's all going to be okay. It's all I've ever done. Even now, I want to do it. I want to trust him, accept what he's saying, and promise everything will be okay. "I know you must hate me, but I can't lose you, Andi. I can't. I'll never survive it."

I stand, almost in a trance, and walk toward him. I can't feel my hands, my feet, my face. It's as if someone else has taken over my body as my husband wraps me in his arms.

I don't want to do this anymore.

I don't want to be that little girl.

That woman.

The apologist, Heidi called me. The *stand by her man* woman.

The one who excuses, overlooks, people pleases, and quiets her voice so others can speak over her. So men can speak over her. Take from her. Control her.

I close my eyes, a tear slipping down my cheek onto the fabric of his shirt.

"I'm sorry," he whispers, rubbing my back.

I slip my hand into my pocket. *I don't want to do this anymore.* "Me too."

He doesn't notice the knife, doesn't see it coming as I rear back and thrust it into his stomach. He cries out, but I don't stop. I can't. I stab my husband, the man I love, over and over and over again.

For the girl. For her mom. For our daughter. For me.

For every little girl or woman who's ever been silenced.

For the little girl I was in the back seat of that car. For the woman I will never be again.

When I release his shoulder, he steps backward, staring down in horror at what I've done.

He shakes his head, tilting his cheek toward his shoulder as if he doesn't understand.

"Andi... You didn't have to..."

He sways, cutting his sentence short as he teeters backward slowly and then all too fast. He slams onto the concrete with a loud *SMACK.* Lying on his back in the puddle of both their blood, he blinks slowly, one hand moving up his stomach. His eyes stare at everything and nothing all at once.

Within minutes, he's gone.

It's over fast. The one merciful thing.

I'm not sure how long I stand there, breathing and existing, processing all that's happened since I left work early thinking something was wrong.

When the fog clears from my mind, I bend down and place the knife in Heidi's hand, a new plan forming in my mind.

"I'm sorry," I whisper. "I protected your daughter. I'm so sorry I wasn't strong enough to protect you."

I hope, wherever she is, she can hear me.

CHAPTER TWENTY

ANDI

When the police arrive, I'm sitting on the couch in the living room.

My body feels like it's stuck inside a block of solid ice. They pull up with their lights flashing, sirens blaring, and within seconds, a swarm of police officers is on my porch.

There are two female officers standing in front of me when I swing the door open. One with a pale complexion and a smattering of freckles across her nose and the other with warm, amber skin and sharp green eyes.

I study them. Stare at them. *Do you know what I've done?*

"Ma'am, we received a call about—"

"Yes," I cut her off, stepping back in a daze. "Come in."

"Is he inside?" she asks before they enter.

"Downstairs." I sniffle.

"Is he armed? Does anyone in the house have a weapon?"

It's what the dispatcher already asked me on the phone.

"No." My chin quivers along with my voice. I'm barely holding it together. "They're both gone. It's...it's just me. The weapons are downstairs...where I found them. Through the kitchen. The door on the left."

"Very good." The partners exchange a glance and, with the wave of a hand over her shoulder, the one with freckles sends the swarm of officers forward into the house.

Their heavy footsteps plod through the living room, then the kitchen, and down the stairs.

We wait.

For a long time, I hear only silence. Then hushed voices.

A hand comes to rest on my shoulder, and I look up, realizing the two officers haven't left me. I didn't notice.

"Before we sit, I should ask if you're hurt?" She stares down at my bloody shirt. I've already told the dispatcher I'm not, so I assume she knows the answer to this. "The EMTs are on their way. We can get you some medical attention."

"No. I'm not hurt. It's... It's my husband's blood."

The officer without freckles steps forward, coaxing me down on the couch with care. She gestures to the chair beside her. "May we?"

"Please." Ordinarily, I'd be worried about whether I'm being rude to them. Now, I can't seem to care about anything at all.

The officer sits down on the ottoman directly in front of me while the officer with freckles takes a seat in the armchair. "Ma'am, I'm Detective Jackson. This is Detective May. We'd like to go over exactly what happened here today when you're ready."

Will I ever be?

I nod, playing with the seam on the side of my jeans. "O-okay."

Detective May pulls out a notebook as Detective Jackson starts in with the questions.

"For the record, we should start with your name."

"Andi—Cassandra. Cassandra Edwards."

She gestures toward the ceiling, spinning her hand in a circle. "Is this your house, Mrs. Edwards?"

She says Mrs., but I guess I'm just a Ms. now, aren't I? How long until I'm used to that?

"Yes. It is."

"And you placed the 9-1-1 call?"

The 911 call. The way she makes it sound, there was only one. None of the neighbors called in about hearing the gunshot. So, I had more time than I thought. Would knowing that before have made a difference? Would I have made a different decision?

"Ma'am?" she prompts.

"Sorry. Yes, I did."

"Who lives here with you?"

"I... My husband and I do. *Did*. Before... Before this. And my kids."

Nothing I'm saying makes sense. I hope she can sort it out through the jumbled mess that has become my mind.

"You, your husband, and your kids? Is that correct?"

"Yes. That's... That's correct."

"And what are their names?"

"My husband is—was—Spencer Edwards. Our kids are Ava and James."

"Same last name?"

"Yes."

His last name.

"And how old are they?"

"Ava's eight. James is six. He just started kindergarten." I don't know why I offer up the information, but she doesn't seem bothered by it. She nods politely and continues.

"And where are your kids right now?"

"They're..." I wring my hands together in my lap. "They're spending the weekend with my friend."

"Your friend?"

"Jo Goldsmith."

"Are you able to give us Ms. Goldsmith's information? We'll want to contact her to confirm this."

"Yes, of course." I rattle off her address and phone number while Detective May writes it down.

I feel as if I'm sinking into an odd sort of emptiness. Quiet. Like a vat of syrup has swallowed me whole. It's the strangest thing.

"Thank you. Do your kids spend time with Ms. Goldsmith often?"

"Occasionally, but not too often on their own. She's their godmother, but they're always home with us unless something comes up and they can't be."

"Like this weekend?"

"Yes. Spencer asked me to let them stay with her this weekend. It was last minute."

She glances at Detective May, then back at me. "Did you think that was odd? What reason did he give for wanting them to stay with Ms. Goldsmith rather than at your house?"

"Not particularly odd, no. He said he was sick. He told me he'd come home from work early with some sort of stomach bug. James manages to catch everything. We didn't want to chance him or his sister catching it. It just seemed like an easy solution."

I can't tell if she believes me. She seems sympathetic, but maybe she can see right through my lies.

She's quiet for a moment, her eyes taking in every inch of my face. "So you asked Ms. Goldsmith to keep them for the weekend?"

"Yes. I called her this afternoon. Before the kids left school."

"Did you tell her why you wanted her to keep them?"

"Yes. I did."

She nods, rubbing her chin for a minute. "So, after you dropped the kids off at Ms. Goldsmith's house, what happened?"

"Actually, it was our sitter who took them to Jo, er, Ms. Goldsmith's house. Kaylee. Our sitter's name is Kaylee Alford. She's a student in my class. We have her pick them up from school every day and then she normally stays here to help with homework and watch them until I get home from work, and sometimes errands, around five or six. She brought the kids home today to pick up their overnight things and drop off their backpacks and then took them to Jo's. Do you need her information, too?"

"Yes. Her phone number and address please. Anyone we can speak to in order to corroborate your story and make sure it's airtight will be helpful."

I swallow. "Of course." Again, I give them her information.

"Thank you. Now, what happened after the sitter took them to Ms. Goldsmith's house?"

"Well, at first, nothing. I stayed in bed and watched TV

for a while. I was staying in a separate bedroom to try to avoid catching the bug, too. Since Spencer had already been in our bedroom when he arrived home, he suggested he remain in our bedroom and I could sleep in the guest room."

"And you were okay with that arrangement?"

"Yeah. It made sense. He didn't actually want me to stay in the house at all. He thought it would be better if I left, but I was scared I'd already been exposed and would just be taking the germs to Jo's, so that was what we finally agreed on. He promised he'd stay in the bedroom."

"And did he?"

"Mostly, yes. He left once after the kids had gone to Jo's. He said he needed to go downtown to pick something up for work."

"Did you think that was strange?"

"I didn't think it was a good idea, but his boss can be kind of difficult, so I understood. He wasn't gone long. After that, I made him promise to stay in his room. If he needed anything, he was supposed to text me, but I never heard anything from him."

"Did you see him at all from the time he returned home until your 9-1-1 call?"

My muscles tense. "Yes. Just once. I brought him water and crackers a few times, but I never went into our room. He told me to leave them at the door. Less exposure that way. And then, at one point—about two hours ago, I guess—he knocked on the door to the guest room and asked if I'd drive to the pharmacy to get him some medicine. He asked me to go to one across town, said it looked like the medicine he wanted wasn't in stock at the one we usually go to, but I decided I'd better check. And I was glad I did because I found some."

"You bought medicine at this pharmacy?"

I press my lips together, nodding. "I did. It's right over there, actually. Still in my purse. Can I get it?" I point to my purse at the end of the couch.

The detectives exchange glances, and finally, Detective Jackson nods.

I reach for my purse, grasp the white plastic bag, and hold it out for her. Before taking it, she puts on a pair of blue gloves from her pocket. She peers into the bag and lifts the receipt and unopened bottle of nausea medicine out.

Quickly, she reads the bottle, then the receipt—complete with a time stamp, further confirming my story—and places them down on the table. "We may have to take this with us."

"It's not like I need it anymore," I whisper, tears welling in my eyes.

She seems to regret her words as we sit in silence. I wipe a hand across each cheek. "I'm so sorry."

"There's no need to apologize, Mrs. Edwards."

Again, I wipe my tears and suck in a breath.

"Are you ready to go on?"

"Yes," I squeak.

"After you bought this medicine"—she points to the bottle sitting next to her—"then what happened?"

"When I got back..." I pause, looking down as new tears fill my eyes.

"Take your time," Detective Jackson says, pulling off her gloves slowly. When I look up, I focus on the collar of her shirt. I can't bear to look her in the eyes.

"When I got back, I heard someone screaming."

"Someone?" The detective straightens, scooting closer to me.

"A woman. I heard what sounded like a woman screaming. It was coming from the basement. Then, I heard a bang. A gunshot."

"What did you hear after that?"

I squint my eyes as if trying to remember. "Nothing at first. Silence. I was so scared. I worried I'd imagined it. I honestly thought maybe I'd managed to catch whatever he had and was hallucinating. But then..." I cover my mouth with my hand as a sob tears through me. "Then I heard him screaming."

"You heard your husband screaming next?"

"Yeah. Yes. More like groaning, I guess. It was...dull. I don't know how else to describe it." My next words come out with breathless honesty. "I can't stop hearing the noises he made."

"What did you do?"

"Well, the door was locked. Or... Well, jammed, maybe. We have so much trouble with the latch. When I couldn't get it open, I panicked. I grabbed a hammer from under the sink and started smashing it. I didn't know what else to do. Once I'd broken the door, I rushed down the stairs. It wasn't the safest thing to do, I guess, but I wasn't thinking. And, when I got down there, I found them."

"I need you to be clear, Mrs. Edwards. When you got down to the basement, what exactly did you see?"

I take a deep breath. "The woman was...she was lying on one of our comforters on the floor. She was still alive, but barely. She was holding a knife in her hand. My husband was lying next to her on his back. He...he wasn't breathing." I lift my hand to my lips, then meet her eyes. "There was so much blood."

"Did you recognize the woman?"

"No, I've never seen her before."

"You're sure?"

"Positive."

"Okay. Once you were down there, what did you do?"

"I tried to save Spencer." I gesture to my bloody shirt and arms. "He was bleeding out, but he wouldn't look at me. I couldn't make myself believe he was gone. It didn't make sense. *Doesn't* make sense. There was a stack of towels in the puddles of blood, still folded, like he'd brought them down there and they'd soaked up the blood. Why would he have them down there?"

"What else did you see, Mrs. Edwards?"

"I...I saw the gun on the floor and pieced together what I could. I think... I think he shot her, but he wouldn't. You have to believe me. He's not a man who could ever hurt anyone."

"Has he ever hurt you, Mrs. Edwards?"

"Never. Never even raised his voice to me. Spencer is— was—the most kind, loving man I know."

"What else did you see?" she presses.

"Like I said, I saw the knife in her hand. Maybe... Maybe she broke in and he shot her. Maybe he thought she was dead and got too close and she... She..." I shake my head, looking away from her. "I'm sorry. I can't make it make sense in my head."

She's still for a moment, waiting for me to compose myself. "Mrs. Edwards, did you recognize the gun that was on your basement floor?"

"Yes. It's Spencer's."

"Where does he keep it?"

"In our closet in a gun safe. Always locked up. He's very careful about it. With...with the kids."

"And what about the knife in the woman's hand? Was it one you recognized?"

"Yes. We have the same set. I didn't think to check if one of ours is missing..." I cast a glance into the kitchen.

"We'll be sure to check," Detective Jackson says. "After you found them, after you tried to save your husband, what happened?"

"I got sick. In the basement. It was all so much... I'm sorry." I rub my forehead, clearing my throat and wiping away a tear. "And then I came upstairs and called 9-1-1."

"You didn't touch anything?"

"I don't think so. It's all such a blur. I touched Spencer and...and the woman's hands. Her wrist, to check for a pulse."

"Did you touch the weapons?"

"Not the gun, no. I don't think I touched the knife, but I may have bumped it when I was checking her pulse. I... I'm sorry, I don't remember." When they find my fingerprints on the knife, it'll be easy enough to explain away. It belongs to me, after all. I've just admitted that. I use them daily.

"That's okay. I want to clarify, until you got home tonight, until you heard the screams, you never heard any strange sounds coming from the basement?"

"No. Never. We don't go down there much. It's all just storage. I've never heard anything other than the pipes banging a bit, but they're old. They've always done that."

She clasps her hands together. "Mrs. Edwards, has your

husband ever had an affair? Or have you ever suspected your husband of having an affair?"

I shake my head slowly. Regretfully. "No. Never. He's always been so perfect. One of the good ones. But now, I don't know what to think. How to explain what happened in that basement." I give a small, sad smile that quickly turns into a sob. "He wouldn't do this, Detective. I have to believe he wouldn't."

She pulls a tissue from the box on the coffee table and hands it to me. I blow my nose and clear my throat, sniffling. "You think he was having an affair, don't you?"

Her expression tells me all I need to know.

I nod, folding my arms across my lap. "How could I not have seen it? How could I not have known?"

"I don't have any proof your husband was having an affair, ma'am."

"But you believe he was?"

She looks down. "Mrs. Edwards, is there anyone I can call for you? A friend you can stay with, maybe? We'll have to ask you not to stay here while it's an active crime scene."

"I can go to Jo's," I tell her. I take a look at my clothes. "But I'll stay in a hotel tonight and clean up first. I don't want the kids to see me like this."

"You're going to be okay, Mrs. Edwards. I know it doesn't feel like it right now, but you will." She leans forward, patting my knee gently.

Tears paint my cheeks as I stare at her, praying it's true.

CHAPTER TWENTY-ONE

ANDI

The news is set to break in one hour, and the police have warned me reporters will start showing up at the house immediately after. I need to get to Jo's to pick the kids up and then leave town as quickly as possible. I want to take the children away before word gets out.

While it's still an active crime scene, I was allowed to stop by the house to take just a few items in a duffel bag that first had to be searched by the police.

Not that they'll find anything.

All the evidence they need is in that basement.

Like I told the detectives, I spent the night in a hotel room to shower and pull myself together. I need to find a brave face to display for the kids. At this point, I'm falling apart every few seconds.

Everything reminds me of him. Of them. Of what I've done.

I want to be brave and strong, and maybe one day, I will be. For the kids, I can fake it. For the kids, I can do anything.

I'm still not sure I understand how this happened. How we got here. How I ended it. I'm not sure I'll ever forgive myself or forgive him, but at least forgiveness is all I have to worry about. Not the kids' safety. Not my job. Our futures. Not our lives.

Once the horror wears off, the kids and I will be able to continue our lives. Maybe not here. Definitely not in that house. But somewhere.

I don't know how I'll ever explain this to them—maybe that's what scares me the most. Telling them the monsters under their beds aren't the ones they should be afraid of. That sometimes the true monsters are the people we love the most. The people we trust never to hurt us.

From where I'm standing in the living room, I can hear the officers downstairs still. They've told me it could be a few days before the scene will be cleared for us to return home. After that, I'll have to hire a crime scene cleaner to make it livable.

Sellable.

We'll take a loss on the house, no doubt, with its history. But with Spencer's life insurance, we'll be okay.

It's all going to be okay. I just have to keep telling myself that.

With my bag in hand, I swing open the front door. I suck in a sharp breath at the sight waiting for me.

"Kaylee?"

Our babysitter stands in front of me dressed in sweats, eyes swollen and red, her long hair pulled up in a bun. She looks as if she's ready to collapse.

"Honey, what is it? What's wrong?"

"The police just called me." She sobs, covering her mouth with one hand.

Ah, I'd forgotten they were going to call her to verify my story. I had no idea they'd tell her why. No idea it would affect her so much if they did.

I hold out an arm, and she falls into my hug, quaking with sobs. "It's going to be okay. We're going to be okay. We'll get through this. Please don't cry."

"It's my fault she was here..." she cries, her voice so low I almost miss it.

"What did you say?" I pull back from her.

"I'm so sorry, Mrs. Edwards. I'm so sorry."

"What are you sorry for, Kaylee? I don't understand what you mean."

"I never meant for anyone to get hurt." She sobs uncontrollably, her hysteria impossible to soothe. "I thought I loved him."

A block of ice slides down my spine.

"What?"

She's not listening to me, still trying to speak through her bawling. "I only told my mom because I thought she was cool. I thought she'd understand."

No.

No.

No.

"I never thought she'd be angry. I never thought she'd come here. I'm so sorry," she cries again.

My knees buckle underneath me without warning, and I crash to the ground, my lungs suddenly incapable of drawing in oxygen.

I'm back in the vat of syrup.

Sinking.

Sinking.

Next to me, Kaylee drops down slowly, weeping for her mom or my husband, I can't be sure which.

Maybe both.

I pull her into my arms, offering what little comfort I can give in my distraught state. My mind, my thoughts, my vision all fracture. I can never tell her what I did to protect her.

I want to say so much. *No*, and *it's not possible*, but also, *I'm sorry. I'm so sorry.*

Mostly: *How is this happening? How is any of this real?*

Heidi's voice echoes in my ears.

She's only seventeen, Andi.

CHAPTER TWENTY-TWO

KAYLEE

TWO YEARS AGO

When he first sits down next to me, I nearly lose it. I'm sure he's a cop. I'm just waiting for him to ask to see my ID.

I'm just in town visiting my mom for a few days, and already I'm going to cause trouble for her. No wonder she abandoned me.

After growing up most of my life not knowing my mom very well, it was a nice surprise when my dad said she wanted me to come visit her in New York. Wanted to reconnect, apparently.

Not that we've done much reconnecting, really. She's always on set. *But* she gave me her credit card and a fake ID and told me I could go anywhere within ten blocks of her apartment, so there's that.

She's like a big sister more than anything. In the

evenings, we talk about boys, paint our nails, and she sympathizes while I complain about Dad.

Last night, I told her I want to move to New York, like her. That I want to become an actress, too. In New York, it feels like anything is possible. I love my dad, don't get me wrong, but sometimes he acts like Nashville is the only city in the world.

I hate how much it hurt him when I told him I want to leave after graduation.

Just three years away.

Feels like a lifetime.

When the man sits down and offers to buy me a drink, I'm flattered. He's cute enough. More than that, he's nervous. Visibly nervous. The thought that I can make a grown man nervous is thrilling.

I don't miss the way he keeps staring at my boobs.

"Are you...here with someone?"

"In New York? Or here at this restaurant?"

"Either. Both."

If I say I'm here with Mom, he could ask how old I am. Instead, I lie, "I'm here visiting friends. Considering moving here permanently. But I'm at this restaurant alone." His brows bounce up. God, he's like a puppy dog. It's the cutest thing I've ever seen. "At least, I was."

He holds out his hand. Are we in a business meeting? "I'm Spencer."

I can't tell him my name. He'll look me up on social media and find out I'm only fifteen. When I take his hand, I simply say, "Spencer. I like that."

The bartender brings us our drinks and he pays, then says, "I'm here for work. Can't stay too long."

I'll bet he's a doctor or a lawyer or something. He's dressed really nice. "That's too bad. What do you do?"

"I'm a talent agent. In town to sign a new client."

Holy cow. I try to hide how impressed I am. "What a coincidence. I'm trying to get into acting."

"You certainly look the part." His eyes fall to my boobs again, and I feel heat creeping up my neck. He's not even trying to hide it. "I'm an agent for musicians, though. I could get you the information for one of my colleagues that works with actresses."

"That would be amazing, Spencer. Thank you."

"Anytime... Actually, I didn't get your name."

Shoot. "It's..." I think fast. "Well, now that you mention it, I'm trying out some stage names. What do you think of Anna?"

It takes him forever to answer. Does he suspect I'm lying? "Hmm... Anna is nice. Not quite special enough for you."

The heat from my neck seeps to my cheeks. "What would you suggest, then?"

"Where are you from?"

"Nashville." I regret the honest answer immediately. Then again, what are the odds he knows much about Nashville or could ever find me there? "And please don't tell me I should call myself Loretta or Dolly." I laugh, then add, "I'm joking." He's not smiling. Was that rude? It was obviously a joke.

"No, I know. It's just... I'm also from Nashville."

My stomach flips. *The freaking odds.* "You're kidding."

"Nope. Born and raised."

"Me too. What are the odds? Some of the only born-and-raised Nashvillians left in the world, and we meet in a New York City bar." Of all the bars in all the cities...

"You don't have much of an accent."

I do all I can to avoid rolling my eyes. If I had a dollar for every time I heard that. As if that terrible Southern twang is something to be proud of. My whole life, I've listened to my mom speak to me on the phone or in her movies. She doesn't have an accent, so I don't want to either. She got out of our hometown. She's living her dream. If I want to, I can be just like her.

"That's on purpose. I hate my accent. It mostly only comes out when I'm drinking or sleepy." It's easier to tell him this than to try and explain the dynamic with my mom. Which reminds me, I should probably make this drink last. If I have any more, who knows what I might accidentally say?

He runs a finger over his cheek. "Okay. Hmm. What about Presley? It's unique. Hearkens back to your Tennessee roots without being on the nose. You could say your mom was a huge fan of Elvis. People would think it was sweet."

"Hearkens, hmm?" What is this guy, like eighty? Who says hearkens anymore? Who *ever* said hearkens? Is that, like, from the Bible or something? "So fancy."

"Presley." I hate it. My grandma had a dog named Presley, and it bit my cheek when I was little. I still have a small scar. "It has a nice ring to it, yeah." I take a drink, avoiding saying much else. "Tell you what, you call me Presley tonight, and I'll see what I think of it."

I don't mean it to come out as sexual as it sounds, but his ears turn bright red in an instant. Oops.

"I can do that."

"Excellent." I lean forward, taking a sip of my drink. Is this really happening?

"Would you...like to have dinner? With me?"

It's happening.

———

IT IS the longest dinner of my life, but Mom isn't supposed to be home until early morning, thanks to a late shoot, which means I can say yes when he asks me to go to his hotel room with him.

I'm not stupid, I know what he means. What he's really asking.

And I'm all for it.

At least he bought me dinner first, unlike the guys at school. He doesn't look at me the way the guys at school look at me. There is an appreciation there I have never gotten from any of those idiots. He finds me interesting. Beautiful. Sexy.

When Spencer kisses me, it feels like I'm his entire world. When we make love, I see stars. I melt into his bed when we're finished, my entire body on fire with electricity. I'm exhausted and sore as we cuddle up together.

I know it's just for one night. I totally get that we'll never see each other again.

Somehow, I think that makes it all the more fun.

CHAPTER TWENTY-THREE

KAYLEE

ONE YEAR AGO

Two weeks after my sixteenth birthday, my teacher, Mrs. Edwards, asks if I would ever consider nannying. I don't have to think about it for long. I just got my first car, but Dad says I have to get a job and pay for the gas money. The timing is perfect.

Besides, I like Mrs. Edwards. I was always a reader growing up, but it wasn't until I started her class that I found the types of books I really love. Mrs. Edwards isn't like the teachers in the movies. We don't have to read boring classics with outdated language that make no sense. Instead, she lets us choose from newer books. Some of my favorites have been *Speak* by Laurie Halse Anderson, *Tears of a Tiger* by Sharon M. Draper, *The Fault in Our Stars* by John Green, and *The Hate U Give* by Angie Thomas. She offers us books that actually mean something and make sense to people my age.

She has two kids, Ava and James, and she and her husband need a sitter for afternoons.

I figure...what's the worst that can happen?

I SPEND a full week on the job before I meet Mr. Edwards. Typically, Mrs. Edwards is the first one home and I leave shortly after, but tonight, she's already warned me she'll be late. I hear his car door shut outside and gather Ava's newly completed homework into a stack.

When the front door opens, the kids go wild. They dart away, immediately choosing him over me.

Cool, kids. Love you, too.

"Daddy!"

"Daddy's home."

"Daddy, Daddy! Guess what I did at school?"

"Hey, buds. What did you do at school, James?"

"Played wizard," James says in an evil sort of voice.

Mr. Edwards laughs. "Ah, I hope you didn't cast any evil spells, Mr. Wizard." He's closer to me now. I hear his shoes on the tile of the kitchen floor. "Oh, hey. You must be Kaylee."

I spin around with Ava's colored pencils in my hands as I struggle to force them in her pouch. "Yeah. I am. So nice to finally meet you, Mr. Ed—" I freeze.

No.

No.

No.

What are the odds?

I have to quit saying that.

He pales. Swallows. Blinks.

I'm *so* going to be fired.

"Nice to finally meet you, too." He places his briefcase on the island and holds out his hand.

I take it, feeling the spark that was there a year ago return in seconds. He walks away without another word. Maybe we'll just pretend it never happened.

Maybe that's best.

WHEN SPENCER WALKS me out to the car that evening, he's nervous. Shifty. He keeps clearing his throat and touching his nose.

I try to prepare myself for what I know is coming. He's going to fire me, and I hate it. As it turns out, I like working for Mrs. Edwards. The pay is great and the kids are so sweet. I don't want to lose this job.

"I won't... I won't tell anyone if that's what you're worried about," I tell him, looking over at him from behind my hair.

He lets out a deep sigh like my dad does before he's about to give me a long lecture about something boring. When Spencer speaks, he keeps his voice low. "Kaylee, you lied to me. You never told me how old you are."

"Technically, I didn't lie."

His eyes narrow, but I can't tell if he looks mad. More worried than anything. Scared maybe. But also...a little playful. I can work with that.

"*What?*" I bat my eyelashes at him, bumping his arm with my shoulder. "I didn't. You never asked."

He stops in his tracks and turns to face me. "You're in high school."

I bite my lip, clutching my purse at my waist. "I know. I'm sorry. It's just...you caught me at a bar drinking. I couldn't very well tell you I was fifteen."

"*Fifteen?* Fuck." He breathes out a sigh, covering his forehead with his palm. "Sorry."

I laugh. "I've heard worse." I narrow my eyes. "From you, actually, as I recall."

"Don't joke about that. I could go to jail. You realize that, right?"

"Relax. I told you I'm never going to tell anyone." I run my fingers across my mouth, zipping my lips up, and pretending to lock them. "You can trust me, Spencer. And for what it's worth, I had a lot of fun that night. It was very" —I glance down, then back up—"memorable."

He looks away, massaging the place between his eyes. I'm not sure where this confidence is coming from, though joining drama club has helped me learn to fake it a bit.

I reach out, tugging playfully at his sleeve. "I never thought I'd see you again. I can't believe this."

When his eyes come back to me, they're full of sadness. Longing. "Me either."

I purse my lips, staring at him with the same look I gave him that night. I fold my arms across my chest and his eyes land on my boobs in a second. He doesn't pull them away. He still wants me, which means I can keep this job. Maybe I can keep him, too.

His eyes flick up to meet mine with a suspicious look, and he twists his lips, checking over his shoulder. Without warning, he starts walking again. "You should go, Kaylee. Before we do something stupid."

I smirk, jogging to keep up with him. "Stupid? Wouldn't dream of it."

When we reach my car, he opens my door and I slip inside.

"So, should I call you Spencer or Mr. E?" I drag out the question, pressing my tongue against my teeth.

"Mr. E," he says softly.

"Is that all the time? Or...just when your wife's around?"

He runs a hand across his mouth. "Kaylee..." he warns.

"Okay, okay. I'm teasing." I grab my seat belt and buckle in.

He's still holding my door open.

I glance up at him. "You gonna let me go?"

"For today, at least." He leans down, his cheeks bright red. "You look good, by the way. The new hair suits you."

"Good to know. I'll keep it." I run a finger over my new, shoulder-length waves. They've just been highlighted.

His hand slips down my arm, lingering for a second too long. When the grin finds his lips, we both know what's coming next.

We can't resist it.

"Our little secret," I whisper. "You can trust me."

He runs his teeth over his bottom lip slowly, staring at me like I'm too good to be true. "You're dangerous, you know it?"

I grin.

What's the worst that could happen?

DON'T MISS THE NEXT DOMESTIC THRILLER FROM KIERSTEN MODGLIN!

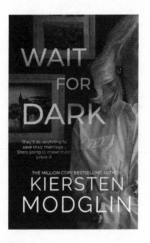

They'll do anything to save their marriage...
She's going to make them prove it.

Purchase *Wait for Dark* today:
https://mybook.to/waitfordark

WOULD YOU RECOMMEND DON'T GO DOWN THERE?

If you enjoyed this story, please consider leaving me a quick review. It doesn't have to be long—just a few words will do. Who knows? Your review might be the thing that encourages a future reader to take a chance on my work!

To leave a review, please visit:
https://mybook.to/DontGoDownThere

Let everyone know how much you loved
Don't Go Down There on Goodreads:
https://bit.ly/dontgodownthere

STAY UP TO DATE ON EVERYTHING KMOD!

Thank you so much for reading this story. I'd love to invite you to sign up for my mailing list and text alerts so we can be sure you don't miss my next release.

Sign up for my mailing list here:
kierstenmodglinauthor.com/nlsignup

Sign up for my text alerts here:
kierstenmodglinauthor.com/textalerts

ACKNOWLEDGMENTS

As always, I should start by thanking my amazing husband and sweet little girl—thank you for believing in me, cheering me on, listening to me whine when plots aren't working, and putting up with my never-ending chatter about stories and characters you haven't met yet. I love you both so very much.

To my wonderful editor, Sarah West—thank you for seeing the story I want to tell through all the mess, for helping me find it, and for always believing I have a story worth telling. I'm so grateful for you.

To the incredible proofreading team at My Brother's Editor, Rosa and Ellie—thank you for your amazing eagle eyes and for polishing my stories until they shine. I'm very thankful to have you on my team.

To my loyal readers (AKA the #KMod Squad)—thank you for believing in me, cheering me on, and always being excited for the next story. As a little girl, I wished for each and every one of you and you are an absolute dream come true.

To my book club/gang/besties—Sara, both Erins, June, Heather, and Dee—thank you for always knowing how to make me laugh, for being excited whenever I have news (no matter how small), and being the highlight of even the hardest weeks. I love you, girls.

To my bestie, Emerald O'Brien—thank you for being my sounding board, my voice of reason, my biggest cheerleader, and the one who knows everything. I love you so much, friend.

To Becca and Lexy—thank you for helping me stay on track, for the hilarious memes that make my day, and for keeping the KMod Squad so much fun.

To Jo Goldsmith, Linda Smith, and Kaylee Alford— sweet readers whose names appeared in this story. Thank you for trusting me with your namesakes. I had so much fun adding them into this world!

Last but certainly not least, to you—thank you for purchasing this book and supporting my art. Whenever I'm writing a story, I'm always thinking of you. I wonder about which plot twists will shock you, which characters you'll root for, and whether this story will live up to the promise I made when you picked up this book. I truly hope it has entertained and kept you guessing every step of the way. And, as always, whether this is your first Kiersten Modglin book or your 37th, I hope it was everything you hoped for and nothing like you expected.

ABOUT THE AUTHOR

KIERSTEN MODGLIN is an Amazon Top 10 bestselling author of psychological thrillers. Her books have sold over a million copies and been translated into multiple languages. Kiersten is a member of International Thriller Writers, Novelists, Inc., and the Alliance of Independent Authors. She is a KDP Select All-Star and a recipient of *ThrillerFix's* Best Psychological Thriller Award, *Suspense Magazine's* Best Book of 2021 Award, a 2022 Silver Falchion for Best Suspense, and a 2022 Silver Falchion for Best Overall Book of 2021. Kiersten grew up in rural western Kentucky and later relocated to Nashville, Tennessee, where she now lives with her family. Kiersten's readers across the world lovingly refer to her as "KMod." A binge-watching expert, psychology fanatic, and *indoor* enthusiast, Kiersten enjoys rainy days spent with her favorite people and evenings with her nose in a book.

Sign up for Kiersten's newsletter here:
kierstenmodglinauthor.com/nlsignup

Sign up for text alerts from Kiersten here:
kierstenmodglinauthor.com/textalerts

kierstenmodglinauthor.com
www.facebook.com/kierstenmodglinauthor
www.facebook.com/groups/kmodsquad
www.twitter.com/kmodglinauthor
www.instagram.com/kierstenmodglinauthor
www.tiktok.com/@kierstenmodglinauthor
www.goodreads.com/kierstenmodglinauthor
www.bookbub.com/authors/kiersten-modglin
www.amazon.com/author/kierstenmodglin

ALSO BY KIERSTEN MODGLIN

<u>STANDALONE NOVELS</u>

Becoming Mrs. Abbott

The List

The Missing Piece

Playing Jenna

The Beginning After

The Better Choice

The Good Neighbors

The Lucky Ones

I Said Yes

The Mother-in-Law

The Dream Job

The Nanny's Secret

The Liar's Wife

My Husband's Secret

The Perfect Getaway

The Roommate

The Missing

Just Married

Our Little Secret

Widow Falls

Missing Daughter

The Reunion

Tell Me the Truth

The Dinner Guests

If You're Reading This...

A Quiet Retreat

The Family Secret

Wait for Dark

ARRANGEMENT TRILOGY

The Arrangement (Book 1)

The Amendment (Book 2)

The Atonement (Book 3)

THE MESSES SERIES

The Cleaner (Book 1)

The Healer (Book 2)

The Liar (Book 3)

The Prisoner (Book 4)

NOVELLAS

The Long Route: A Lover's Landing Novella

The Stranger in the Woods: A Crimson Falls Novella